BERLIN
EXCHANGE

Recent Titles by Ted Allbeury from Severn House

BERLIN EXCHANGE ✓
CODEWORD CROMWELL ✓
THE GIRL FROM ADDIS
THE LANTERN NETWORK
THE LONELY MARGINS

BERLIN
EXCHANGE

Ted Allbeury

This title first published in Great Britain 2000 by
SEVERN HOUSE PUBLISHERS LTD of
9–15 High Street, Sutton, Surrey SM1 1DF.
Originally published 1987 in Great Britain by
New English Library under the title *The Crossing*.
This title first published in the USA 2000 by
SEVERN HOUSE PUBLISHERS INC., of
595 Madison Avenue, New York, NY 10022,

British Library Cataloguing in Publication Data

Allbeury, Ted, 1917-
Berlin exchange
1. Spy stories
I. Title
823.9'14 [F]

ISBN 0-7278-5536-0

687653

MORAY COUNCIL

DEPARTMENT OF TECHNICAL

& LEISURE SERVICES

F

Printed and bound in Great Britain by
MPG Books Ltd, Bodmin, Cornwall.

Foreword

I felt that it was time that I wrote a story about what so-called spies are *really* like. There are no such things as spies, of course, but there are ordinary people who are used for finding out what the enemy are up to.

I love Sean Connery but I wouldn't have him on my team. Far too handsome, far too charming, he'd stand out in a crowd like – well, Sean Connery. I want people who won't be noticed.

This story is about a KGB man in New York and a couple of 'spies' here in England. What I've written for you is virtually true. Even their names are their real names. They haven't got a gun between them and wouldn't know a Walther PPK from a Smith and Wesson revolver.

The guy in New York spends his time trying to be an artist and improve his guitar playing. The couple in England are middle-aged and inoffensive, the husband keeps a bookshop in London.

Nevertheless, these people are all intelligence agents for Soviet intelligence – the KGB. What I've written is what really happened, what it's really like to be a 'spy'. I hope you enjoy it.

Ted Allbeury
January 2000

Part One

1

The boy and the young man were the only people on board the ship. They stood leaning over the rails looking at the crowd around the man standing on the wooden box, waving his arms and shouting, but the sharp wind carried his words away.

'What's he saying, Boris?'

'He's from the Military Revolutionary Committee from the Petrograd Soviet. He's telling them that the workers, the peasants, and the soldiers are in charge now in Russia. All peasants will be given land, the soldiers will be paid and the people will be fed and given jobs.'

'Are they pleased about that?'

The young man laughed. 'They've heard it too many times, boy, from too many people. They don't believe him. They say they want deeds not words.'

The boy looked at the young man's face, tanned and lined from wind and sun. He had strange eyes. Old, sad eyes that never blinked.

'Somebody told me that hundreds of people have been killed, maybe thousands,' the boy said.

The young man nodded. 'And many more thousands will die before all this is over.'

'Why do they kill working people if they want to give them freedom?'

The young man spat over the side of the ship. 'They don't intend to give them freedom, Josef. This is just a struggle for power. Revolutionaries against revolutionaries. Old allies facing the final truth. Which pigs will have their snouts in the trough for the next hundred years. Bolsheviks or Mensheviks.'

'Whose side are you on? Who do you want to win?'

'I'm on the side of whoever wins, boy. And that will be the Bolsheviks. Nobody wants them to win but they will, because they know what they want and they'll kill anyone who stands in their way.'

'Who are these Bolsheviks?'

'Who knows? Here in Petrograd it's Trotsky, Stalin, Sverdlov, Dzerzhinski, Latsis and Peters.'

'How do you know so much about them?'

'I live here. This is my home town. I read the papers and listen to the talk in the bars.'

'Will there be another revolution like they had before?'

'A revolution, yes. But not like we've had before. This time it is power-hungry men at each other's throats. The people will be safe until it's over.'

'When will it be decided who's won?'

'Tonight, at the meeting of the MRC. Tomorrow we shall have new Tsars, in the pay of the Germans this time.'

It was October 25, 1917.

Misha had been a worker in one of the iron-foundries. He was one of Zagorsky's friends and the young man let him on board once or twice a week so that he could have a meal. There was neither bread nor vegetables any longer in the whole of Petrograd despite the promises of commissars from the revolutionary committees.

Even on the ship there were only the standard tins of bully-beef and not enough of those to offer to anybody who wasn't a member of the crew. The meal the three of them ate was boiled potatoes in a thin Oxo cube gravy. Misha ate it with obvious relish, Zagorsky ate it without noticing and young Josef was too busy talking to notice what he was eating.

'Tell me what else they're going to do, Misha.'

'Every man will be free. No more serfs. No more peasants. Every farmer with his own land. No Cossacks to

4

ride down the people. No policeman can arrest a worker without a reason. Laws that protect every citizen.

'We shall share everything; food, housing, work, goods. Every man will care for his neighbour, and all will be equal. No Tsars. No more Rasputins. No priests. For us we work today for our children's tomorrow. And our children's children.' He waved his arms. 'A workers' paradise, young Josef.'

The boy smiled. 'You really think they will do all these things, Misha?'

'I swear it, boy. On my heart and on my soul. It will take time to sort out the past but they are making the laws now.' He tapped the table with his spoon. 'At this minute Lenin is planning Russia's wonderful future. We are a great people. They have freed our greatness. It will happen.'

Zagorsky grinned. 'That's what they said when the women came out in 1905 in Vyborg District, shouting for bread. Kerensky said it years ago. Mentov wrote it in *Iskra* six months ago.'

'That's the point, my friend. The Military Revolutionary Committee was split between the Mensheviks and the Bolsheviks. The Mensheviks promised but did nothing, the Bolsheviks are not afraid. They fought for us. They organised the revolution.'

Zagorsky laughed. 'All the pigs are fighting for power. We'll see. You'd better get back to your place or they might give it to some deserving Bolshevik.'

Misha rose easily to the taunt, beating his fist against his thin chest. 'I am a Bolshevik, my friend.'

The boy walked to the companionway with Misha and pulled aside the rough gate that kept unauthorised people off the boat.

The Russian turned to the boy. 'You care, don't you, Josef? You understand our joy.'

The boy smiled. 'Yes, I understand, Misha. Zag just likes teasing you.'

'He is no fool, that fellow. He knows a lot. He listens

5

and watches. He knows much more than he says. But he has no heart.' Misha smiled. 'Not like us, my friend. We are comrades, yes?'

'Of course, Misha.'

Back in the saloon the boy collected up the dishes and took them to the small galley. As he dried the last enamel plate Zagorsky walked in and sat on the small box that held the cleaning materials.

'Did you believe what Misha said?'

The boy hesitated, blushing. 'Why not? What he says makes sense.'

'They will work harder than they've ever worked in their lazy lives and for no more money. It will take years before any of it comes true.'

'So? What does it matter? They make sacrifices for their children's sake. It's like planting seeds. You have to wait for the corn to grow.'

Zagorsky laughed. 'Who said that, boy?'

'Said what?'

'About planting seeds.'

'I said it. It's true.'

'Would you do all that if there was a revolution in England?'

'Of course I would. All workers would.' He frowned. 'But there's no chance of a revolution in England.'

'Maybe one day you'll have the chance. You'd fight with the workers, would you?'

'Of course.'

Zagorsky said softly, 'Why don't you stay here in Petrograd and help? It would be good experience for when your time comes.'

'I've signed on, Zag; I'd go to prison if I jumped ship.'

'They'll never have the chance, boy, if you stay. You could walk off now and nobody could stop you.'

'There's Royal Navy ratings at the dockyard gates.'

'So we don't go out through the gates.'

'But you don't believe in it, Zag. You think they won't do it.'

6

The young man looked at the boy a long time before he spoke, and then he said, 'Never believe what a man says, no matter who he is. Listen, but don't believe. Listen for what's believed in, what's in his mind. That's *all* that matters.' He paused. 'Do you want to stay and help? It will be hard work, with lots of disappointments.'

'Would I be with you and Misha?'

'Maybe. But you've got to learn the language first. Not many Russians speak English, especially the kind you'd be working with.'

'Would they have me?'

Zagorsky nodded. 'Yes. They'd have you. We need all the help we can get. Think about it tonight. If tomorrow you still want to help I'll take you to see the right people.'

'But what good will I be? I can't do anything.'

'I've watched you, Josef. You are a good organiser – and you're honest. That's enough.'

After three months the boy they called Josef could speak enough Russian to understand the orders he got and to hold a reasonable conversation. The Russian he learned was crude and ungrammatical, like the speech of his fellow workers. He saw Misha most days but seldom saw Zagorsky. He realised from what people said that the young man he called Zag so familiarly was important. Zag went to meetings of the Council of People's Commissars, the *sovnavkom*, and mixed with leaders like Lenin and Dzerzhinski, who was the head of the newly formed Committee for Struggle Against the Counter-Revolution. The committee that became what people called the *Cheka*.

The boy learned his way around the backstreets of Petrograd, carrying messages and delivering batches of the latest issue of *Pravda*. At night he sat listening to the heated discussions on how long the Bolsheviks would last. Some gave them only a few days, others a month or

7

two and a few, very few, said that the Bolsheviks would be the final victors in the ruthless struggle for power that was being waged in the Duma.

By December 1917 the Bolsheviks had taken control. Arrests, confiscations and house searches were common and there were numerous cases of violence by self-appointed bandit-revolutionaries. Drunkenness and disorder were widespread in the city and rumour had it that it was much the same in all big cities. A newspaper published a speech by Maxim Gorky which said openly that the Bolsheviks were already showing how they meant to rule the country. His final sentence was, 'Does not Lenin's government, as the Romanov government did, seize and drag off to prison all those who think differently?' But no figure arose who could successfully stop the ruthless surge to power of Lenin's men. Resistance from any quarter was met by bringing out the workers on the streets. They seldom knew what they were demonstrating about but it had become part of their daily lives. For the Bolsheviks it was a warning to all those who opposed them that 'power lay in the streets'.

There was a wide spectrum of resistance to the Bolsheviks, including many workers' groups and political parties; almost all left-wing political parties were sworn enemies who recognised that the Bolsheviks' struggle for power was just that, and no more. It was like a juggernaut out of control, its only policy repression of the opposition.

Josef saw Misha almost every evening. Misha liked the long rambling discussions that the group fell into every night. Analyses of personalities and policies, forecasts of a golden future or prophecies that nothing would change except a different group of despots who would behave like any Tsar. The boy always remembered Zagorsky's advice. He listened and said nothing, watching their faces, sometimes recognising the false ring of praise for the new leaders from some obviously ambitious man. And

8

sometimes he heard the echo of the deliberate incitement of an *agent provocateur*.

It was a hot summer evening when he had to deliver a letter to Zagorsky and he had been invited in, the Russian pointing to a wooden box that was used as a chair.

'Sit down, Josef. I want to talk to you.'

When Josef was perched on the box Zagorsky looked at his face.

'Are you busy with your errands?'

'Yes.'

'They tell me you can write in Russian now.'

'Not very well.'

'Well enough to make notes of the decisions at the committee meetings, yes?'

'Yes, I do that.'

'Misha thinks you should be made secretary of the committee. Official secretary. How would you feel about that?'

'What would the older men think?'

'What they think doesn't matter. What about you? Do you want to do it?'

'Yes, if it will help.'

'Help what?'

'The revolution. The workers' new freedom.'

Zagorsky half-smiled. 'What do they think of Comrade Lenin down there?'

'Some say he is the only leader who will do what he says. Others say that he is as bad as the Tsar. Some say he is worse.'

'And you? What do you think?'

'I don't know, Comrade Zagorsky. I only hear what others say about him.'

'Comrade, eh? A Bolshevik already?'

The boy smiled, embarrassed. 'At least they are doing things, not just talking about it.'

'Before you are appointed as secretary you will have some training on how to run meetings and control events.

9

It will be in Moscow and it will take about four months. Come and see me tomorrow at ten o'clock, ready to leave.'

'Yes, comrade.'

Josef had had his seventeenth birthday while he was on the training course. Despite being a foreigner he was very popular with the other students. Their ages ranged from eighteen to the mid-fifties and they came from all parts of the Soviet Union. On his birthday they threw a party to celebrate. It was at the party that he met Anna, an eighteen-year-old from Warsaw. Polish and proud of it, her father had been a party worker for many years. She too was going to be secretary to a committee in Moscow.

They were housed in an old warehouse just across the Moscow River in Kuncevo. The building was divided up into classrooms, sleeping accommodation and a canteen that provided only very basic meals of vegetable soup and bread. Twice a week there were special rations of potatoes.

Josef found some of the people on the course strange to the point of being mentally unbalanced. Men who were fanatics, constantly leaping to their feet and quoting from Marx and Lenin. Arguing with the instructors at every opportunity. Smug and self-satisfied, pleased with the divisiveness of their disruption. But most of the students were working-class men and women whose only concern was to learn how to be competent leaders in some small committee and help their fellow workers improve their standards of living.

Josef and Anna were both model students, but on fine evenings they walked along the river bank and stared across at the island and Terechovo. They were cautious at first about what they said but as time went by they talked, guardedly but honestly.

'Why is an Englishman interested in a revolution in Russia?'

'Because I'm working-class and I think workers get a

poor deal all over the world. I wish there could be a revolution in England.'

'You could go back and start one yourself.'

'Things aren't as bad there for workers as they are here. They're not ready for a revolution.'

'Levkin the instructor said that you had the right kind of mind to be an organiser. He said you were to be trusted and you learned quickly.'

'Did you ask him about me?'

'Yes.'

'Why?'

'Because I'm staying on for another month of training. I suggested that you should stay on too.'

'I've got work to do when I get back to Petrograd.'

'This is special training. Only for trusted people. Comrade Zagorsky had recommended you for further training.'

'Why do you want me to stay on here?'

'Because I shall miss you. I like being with you.'

He smiled and reached for her hand. 'I like being with you but I didn't have the courage to tell you.'

'You didn't need to tell me. I knew.'

'How could you tell?'

'When you talk to me your voice is different. It's gentle and deep. You don't paw me like other men try to do.'

'Which men?'

'Don't be angry, Josef. And don't be jealous. I can look after myself.' She paused. 'So will you stay if they want you to?'

'If Zag wants me to and if you want me to then I'll stay.'

'You shouldn't call him Zag. He's a very important man now. He's a commissar at the new Ministry of Foreign Affairs.'

He laughed. 'He won't mind what I call him.'

'How did you get to know him so well?'

'I was cabin-boy on a British boat that was tied up in Petrograd when the revolution started. People came to

11

arrest the crew in case they were spies. I was left with Zag to guard the ship against looters.'
'Did he talk you into staying?'
'No. He was very critical of . . .' He shrugged, '. . . no, I wanted to stay.'

Josef never went back to his old committee in Petrograd. After the extension course he was sent as secretary to a committee in one of the Moscow suburbs. Anna went as an administrator to the security organisation, the Ve-Cheka, which controlled all local Chekas throughout the Soviet Union. Its chief was Feliks Edmundovich Dzerzhinski, an austere and ruthless man who came from an aristocratic Polish family.

Josef and Anna saw one another regularly during the following six months. They recognised the dangers of talking about their work even to one another. Zagorsky was now even more important and he seemed to go out of his way to encourage their relationship. When they decided they wanted to live together it was Zagorsky who used his influence to get them a room in a new block of workers' flats.

It was in August 1918 that Josef was called to the building that had once been the offices of the All-Russia Insurance Company and had now been taken over by the Party. Three men interviewed him. One of them was Zagorsky. They asked him question after question about his background in England and his work in Petrograd and Moscow. When he left he had no idea what the purpose of the meeting had been. It was two months later that he heard he was being transferred as an administrator to the Cheka division which Zagorsky controlled. The Secret Political Department.

By that time the Cheka was quite plainly an instrument of brutal power which was outside any legal control, and was used openly to suppress even the mildest resistance to the regime. Imprisonment without trial, on speculation alone, and liquidation when necessary, were its normal weapons against the people. Apart from political suppression, personal rivalries and old scores were being settled by the newcomers to power.

It was a stifling summer evening in their small room when Anna told him that she was pregnant. As soon as she saw that Josef was delighted with the news she was happy too. They had a state wedding a month later. Zagorsky had smiled and said that they were two little bourgeois, not real Bolsheviks, but he had come to the brief ceremony together with half a dozen of their friends. Afterwards they had all had tea and cakes in their room.

When Anna stopped working, a month before their child was due, it gave them more time together and they walked every day to the local park and watched the mothers with their babies and the old *babushkas* who looked after toddlers while their mothers were at work.

One day they sat there for ten minutes without speaking and then Josef said, 'Are you feeling all right?'

'Yes.'

She smiled. 'I'm fine. I can't wait for it to arrive.'

'You seem very quiet these last few days.'

'Do I?'

Josef noticed the evasion. 'Is there anything else troubling you?'

She nodded as she looked at his face. 'I don't want to go back to that place.'

'Why not?'

'I don't like the things they do.'

'What kind of things?'

'You must know what they do, Josef, you work there too.'

'What things do you dislike?'

'They treat the people like they were enemies. Not just the counter-revolutionaries but ordinary people. There are thousands of people being arrested every month.'

'There's a constitution now, Anna. State laws that govern what can be done.'

'They're not interested in the constitution. They don't

13

care about the laws. Most people arrested never get to a court. And if they do then the Cheka tell the judge what his verdict has to be.'

'They just want to make sure that the revolution is not destroyed by counter-revolutionaries. It will get back to normal when things have settled down.'

'But it's been almost two years now, Josef, and it's getting worse not better. They haven't done the things they promised. None of them.'

'It has taken longer to remove the kulaks than anybody expected. Until that's done there is no land to give to the peasants.'

She shook her head slowly. 'They've taken tens of thousands of hectares from the kulaks in the Ukraine alone. The peasants have been given none of it. They work on collective farms owned by the State. They've just exchanged one set of masters for another.'

'You don't say those kinds of things to other people, do you, Anna?'

'Of course I don't. I'm not a fool.'

'Is there anything else that worries you?'

'I want to go back to Poland, Josef. I can feel at home there. There aren't the same problems.'

'There are plenty of problems in Poland, my love.'

'I know, but they're only the problems that all countries have.'

'They'd never let us go to Poland, Anna. We know too much.'

She looked at his face. 'And what we know is bad for the Bolsheviks, isn't it?'

Josef sighed and looked towards the children playing by the small ornamental lake. 'I'm afraid you're right.'

'You feel the same way I do, don't you?'

'Not really. There's a difference. This isn't my country. I don't feel responsible for what they do.'

'But you know that these people are evil men?'

'Not even that, Anna. I know that they are ruthless and unjust in many ways. But I've always felt that they

14

mean well. They will carry out their promises when the country is organised, settled down. The problems are so big, Anna. Even the fact that they are trying to put things right means that they deserve our sympathy and our support.'

'You must decide what you think, Jo-jo. As long as I don't have to go back to that dreadful place.'

'I'll think of some story, Anna, and I'll see what I can do with Zagorsky.'

'You won't tell him what I've said, will you?'

'Of course I won't.' He smiled and took her arm. 'Let's go back and I'll make us a meal.'

Zagorsky had arranged for her to have the baby in hospital. A rare privilege but one that Josef's hard work justified.

Josef took flowers to her and was allowed to hold the baby who lay contentedly in his father's arms, the big, pale blue eyes like his father's eyes, his neat nose like his mother's.

For several months the new baby had occupied their minds and then Anna's official maternity leave came to an end

Zagorsky listened in silence as Josef explained that Anna wanted to stay on leave for another six months to be with their child. When his lame explanation was finished Zagorsky looked at him.

'Why do you lie to me, Josef?'

'It's not a lie, Comrade Zagorsky. She wants to be at home.'

'That's just another way of saying that she doesn't want to be here. She is more interested in the child than her work.'

'I think there is that too.'

'So why didn't you say so?'

'I didn't want you or the Party to feel that she was discontented.'

15

'Josef, she has been discontented for the last six months.'

'You mean she has said so?'

'No.'

'Her work is not to the standard you expect?'

'Her work is well done, she is conscientious and she carries out her orders meticulously.'

'So what is wrong?'

'I didn't say anything was wrong.' Zagorsky shifted in his chair and looked back at Josef. 'I told you a long time ago not to believe men's words. With some people they show their discontent or unhappiness by working harder and longer than anyone could reasonably expect. Over-compensation for inner feelings of guilt.'

'Guilt of what?'

'Their lack of faith. In this case, lack of faith in the correctness of what she is doing. Or maybe the correctness of what others are doing with whom she is connected.'

'I don't think . . .'

Zagorsky waved his hand to silence him.

'There is another thing, isn't there? Another thing that occupies her mind, not just the child.'

'I don't think so.'

'You've not heard her when she's bouncing the boy on her knee? Crooning away in Polish – "*Jedzie, jedzie, pan, pan – Na koniku, sam, sam . . .*".' He shrugged. 'She even has the boldness to address me at the office in Polish. And that doesn't do her a lot of good with senior people. Nor me either.'

'There's no law against speaking Polish so far as I know.'

The aggressive defence of the girl confirmed Zagorsky's guess that Josef knew all about Anna's attitude to Moscow and the Party.

'Don't play the committee secretary with me, my friend. It won't work.' Zagorsky slammed his fist on the table. 'I want her back here in the department no later than next week. You understand?'

16

'Yes, Comrade Zagorsky.'

'She is entitled to use the crèche. The child will be properly cared for while she is working.'

Two months later they were notified that both of them were being transferred to Warsaw to work with the Polish Bolsheviks, Josef as liaison with the Polish section in Moscow and Anna as secretary to the Commissar for Internal Affairs.

Josef's liaison point in Moscow was Zagorsky. It was not an easy relationship and Zagorsky seemed to go out of his way to keep their meetings formal; showing no signs of any personal friendship. Although it was obviously he who had arranged their assignment to Warsaw. The years of struggle and imprisonment were finally beginning to take their toll on him. He was only five years older than Josef but he looked much older.

They had the top floor of a small house in the centre of Warsaw and Anna had time to make it comfortable and there was room for a small bed for the toddler.

Their lives were very different from their time in Moscow. They had few contacts away from the Party and they were part of an underground movement that was being constantly harassed by the Polish government whose hatred for Moscow was traditional and bitter.

There were new problems for Anna who daily recorded the Bolshevik plans for the overthrow of the Polish government. Meetings where men coldly and calmly discussed the assassination of the President of Poland, Pilsudski, and the planning to turn Poland into another Soviet state disturbed her. She found herself suddenly more patriotic and nationalist than she had ever thought possible in her first surge of enthusiasm for the reforms in Russia. What was good for the virtual slave population of that sprawling continent seemed obscenely inappropriate to a civilised culture that was determinedly Western not Slav. Even in Russia there were still large armed forces actively fighting Moscow for the independence of the

17

Baltic States and the Ukraine and Transcaucasia. And when in the spring of 1920 Moscow offered Poland a peace treaty, the Polish government saw it as a sign of Moscow's weakness and a chance to ensure Polish independence by fostering the independence of Lithuanian, Belorussian and Ukrainian states.

On April 25, 1920, in agreement with the weak government in Kiev, Polish forces launched a surprise attack into the Ukraine. It met little resistance and by May 6 Kiev was occupied by Polish forces.

But the foreign invasion invoked a patriotic upsurge against the Polish invaders and in the space of a month the Polish forces were pushed back to their own borders and beyond. Moscow saw its success as the herald of a communist Poland and in a small town in occupied Poland Feliks Dzerzhinski was set up as the supreme Bolshevik authority in Poland. But the spread of Communism in Poland was a dismal failure and in Moscow the blame for the lack of success had to be allotted, not only for that failure but for the lack of warning about the Polish invasion of the Ukraine. It was easier, and to some extent logical, to heap the blame onto the shoulders of Moscow's Poles rather than its Russians.

When Josef opened the envelope that one of the committee had brought from Moscow the message inside was chilling. It said briefly that they were both wanted urgently in Moscow for discussions. His hands trembled as he folded the half-sheet of paper and tucked it into his jacket pocket. They made arrangements to leave the next day and arrived in Moscow that night. An official from the Internal Affairs department met them at the station, and from him they learned that Zagorsky had been arrested. When they asked what he had been charged with the man merely shrugged. They were taken to a hostel and given a room. There was just a mattress on the floor.

They were careful to say nothing to each other of any significance and they lay with their son between them. It was already getting light the next morning before either of them slept.

Josef sat with their son on a bench outside the room where Anna had been taken and it was three hours before she came out, her face white and tear-stained. A Cheka officer stopped them from speaking to one another and pushed Josef roughly to the door of the room, knocked and waved him inside. There was a militiaman on each side of him as he stood facing the three men sitting at the trestle table. The man in the centre looked down at his papers and then at Josef.

'You are a friend of Boris Zagorsky?'

'Yes.'

'How long have you known him?'

'Since October 1917.'

'How did you meet him?'

'I was cabin-boy on a British ship berthed in the docks at Petrograd. The crew had been arrested by the docks committee; Comrade Zagorsky and I were left to guard the ship.'

'Did he talk politics with you?'

'Yes.'

'Tell us what he said. An overall impression.'

'He was very pro-Bolshevik. He said that the Bolsheviks would take over and put the country right.'

'Why did you join the Party?'

'Because Comrade Zagorsky said I could help in the struggle.'

The man looked down at his papers and then back at Josef.

'When did he start criticising the Party?'

'I never heard him criticise the Party.'

'How did you come to work for him?'

'I was ordered to by the Party.'

'Your wife is Polish?'

19

'Yes. She is also a member of the Party.'

'You knew that Zagorsky was Polish?'

'I heard that he was. He didn't mention it himself.'

'Why did you stay in this country?'

'I told you. Comrade Zagorsky said I would be of use and I wanted to help, so I stayed.'

'Why did you continue to stay? Why are you still here?'

'Because this is where I belong.'

'What about your family in England?'

'I have no family in England. I was an orphan. I lived at an orphanage.'

'When do you intend to return to England?'

Josef shrugged. 'I had never thought of returning to England.'

'Who gave you permission to stay here?'

'Nobody. I joined the Party and I was given work to do.'

'Do you share your wife's views on political matters?'

'We are both Bolsheviks, we have no need to discuss our views.'

'But she defends Zagorsky's actions.'

'I don't know what actions you refer to.'

'You mean that after all your training you were not able to recognise that Zagorsky was a counter-revolutionary? A traitor, more concerned with the politics of Poland than the security of the Soviet Union?'

'I have seen no evidence that would suggest that he was anything but a loyal Party member.'

'Are you a loyal Party member?'

'Of course.'

'Can you prove that?'

'I don't know any way of proving it. But it's a fact.'

'Would you work for the Party in England?'

For only a moment he hesitated and then his training took over.

'I would do anything to establish a fair distribution of work and wealth for the proletariat in Britain.'

20

'Zagorsky will be tried by the People's Court tomorrow. Both you and your wife will attend. We may need you as witnesses. If not you will do well to observe what happens to enemies of the people.'

They said nothing to each other about the interviews while they were in the hostel but as they walked the next day to the Cheka buildings he said softly, 'Did you make any mistakes at your interview?'

'Only one, I think.'

'What was that?'

'I said that Poland was my country even if I was a Bolshevik. I said that it was possible to be a loyal Bolshevik and a loyal Pole as well.'

'That was stupid, Anna.'

'They provoked me. They referred to Poles as savages. I couldn't let them get away with that.'

'You should let them get away with anything. It's just words. And words don't matter.' He paused. 'If they make us witnesses, don't say anything like that in court.'

'You want me to act like a coward, for God's sake?'

'No. Not for God's sake. For our sake and the boy's sake. We can think of what to do when this is all over.'

The panelled room held no more than two dozen people, and most of those were officials. Josef was surprised to see that the five judges were all in army officers' uniforms. So was the prosecutor. The defence lawyer, a civilian, was sitting at a small table, his arms folded across his chest, his eyes closed. There were several policemen and soldiers in the court and on a bench below the tall windows were several civilians. Josef recognised two of them from the committee in Petrograd.

The senior of the judges rapped the gavel on the block and the prosecutor stood up, a sheaf of papers in his hand. And only then did the door at the back of the hall open and Zagorsky was led through to the witness box by a uniformed policeman.

The charge was read out. It merely accused him of being an enemy of the State. There were no specific examples or indications of what sort of evidence would be offered to the court.

As Josef looked across the courtroom at Zagorsky he saw him standing there, one hand pressed to his back as if to relieve a pain and Josef guessed that they'd beaten him across his kidneys. It didn't make too much of a visible bruise but the damage inside was always extreme. Zagorsky stood bent as if he were unable to stand up straight, and his left hand clutched the rail of the witness stand as if to keep himself from falling forward.

The prosecutor made no attempt to establish a coherent case; witnesses were called who quoted what seemed to be quite innocuous criticisms of Party officials who were not meeting Zagorsky's high standards of performance. His Polish origins were established but not emphasised, and the status of the five witnesses was no more than routine clerks and minor administrators in Zagorsky's department. The Polish invasion of Kiev was mentioned but not dwelt on, and an hour after he had started the prosecuting lawyer sat down. He had demanded the death penalty for persistent and secret subversion of the security of the State.

When the defence lawyer rose to his feet Zagorsky's voice rang out, surprisingly loud.

'Dismiss this man. I am defending myself.'

There was a whispered conversation among the judges and the senior officer said that the court would note that Zagorsky had refused the legal aid provided by the State. But if Zagorsky wished to conduct his own case the court would hear him.

Josef had noticed that like the men who had interrogated him they referred to him as Zagorsky not as Comrade Zagorsky or Commissar Zagorsky which was his actual status. They were already distancing him from the Party.

Zagorsky took a deep breath and his voice was clear although he spoke very slowly.

'I quote from the rules of the Communist Party of the Soviet Union. Paragraph four – I quote – "the promotion, in every possible way, of inner-party democracy, the activity and initiative of the Communists, criticism and self-criticism".

'I quote from the same document Part One clause three sub-clauses b and c. I quote – "A party member has the right to discuss freely questions of the Party's policies and practical activities at Party meetings, conferences and congresses, at the meetings of Party committees and in the Party press; to table motions; openly to express and uphold his opinion as long as the Party organisation concerned has not adopted a decision; to criticise any Communist, irrespective of the position he holds, at Party meetings, conferences and congresses, and at the full meetings of Party committees. Those who commit the offence of suppressing criticism or victimising anyone for criticism are responsible to and will be penalised by the Party, to the point of expulsion from the CPSU".'

He paused and he was shaking visibly, his whole body trembling as if tormented by an ague.

'That is all I have to say. That is all that needs to be said. This trial is a farce and the laws of the Soviet Union are being abused in this process. The evidence of the poltroons you bring as witnesses shows how hopeless this prosecution must be.' He paused and closed his eyes. When he opened them again he said, 'You will see that I am trembling, comrades. Make no mistake. I do not tremble from fear. Not even from illness. Oh, no. I tremble because I have been beaten near to death to make me give false evidence that would incriminate me. All my life I have worked loyally for the Party. I ask that those who know me and know my record will step in and punish those people who have so infamously brought this case to the court. I ask not for mercy but for justice. The justice that I sought for all of us when I first walked with my fellow-workers holding that beautiful red flag above our heads. You may cause my death but it will not be execution – it will be murder. Murder from others' greed, jealousy and ambition.' He seemed to hesitate before his final words, gulping for air before he said, 'People in the pay of our enemies, the Germans.'

There was a sudden murmur in the courtroom, quickly stopped by the angry face of the senior judge. He kept his eyes away from Zagorsky as he said, 'The judgement of the People's Court will be promulgated after due consideration.'

The officers stood up and filed to the door and Josef and Anna saw two policemen carry Zagorsky from the witness box. They handled him quite gently.

Outside it was beginning to rain and Josef was glad that it was, so that the rain could hide the tears on Anna's face.

Despite her anxiety to get back to their son she had insisted that they went to the church at the back of the museum. And there she prayed and wept, with Josef standing awkwardly beside her, his hand just touching her shoulder.

They went back to Warsaw and they heard rumours that Zagorsky had been sent to one of the Siberian labour-camps and other rumours that he had been shot the same day, after the trial, at the Lubyanka building.

The treatment meted out to Zagorsky and the totally spurious trial frightened and angered them both. They said nothing to anybody about their feelings. Even between themselves there was a reluctance to admit their disillusion with the Party.

The breaking point came when Anna had to take notes of a meeting where the annexation of Poland was being recommended. Half of Poland would become the Polish Soviet State and a rump would be left that the planners were willing to leave to be annexed in due course by Germany. Hearing Poles describe the annexation of their own country, and listening to the details of how its

24

industry and agriculture would serve the Soviet Union had sickened her.

They walked the streets of Warsaw that night, Josef carrying the small boy in his arms as they talked. Anna wanted to get away, anywhere, and quickly. Josef knew that there was no chance of planning their escape. Anna wouldn't be able to dissemble her feelings long enough. She was ready to carry on for a few days, but no longer. He told her that they would leave at the weekend, starting their journey on the Friday night. If anyone saw them they would say they were having a weekend break in the country.

There was little preparation that Josef could make. They would have to leave their few possessions behind them. But fortunately, like most underground party members, he had always kept their meagre savings in cash, and they both had Soviet passports. He still had his British passport and he tucked their marriage certificate inside it.

Josef bought tickets for only the journey from Warsaw to Łodz. And there he booked them onto the night train to Berlin. At the German frontier there were no problems when they presented their USSR passports. In Berlin they found a cheap lodging house. Josef calculated that he had enough money for them to live frugally for six weeks while they decided what to do.

After a few days Josef realised that because he didn't speak German it was going to be difficult to find work. His Russian and smattering of Polish he was afraid to use in case there were local Party members who would check up on him and cause trouble. Having worked in the Cheka he knew that it had its people in every big European city. As the days went by he became desperate for anything that would provide some income. It was then that he took a job as a dish-washer in the kitchens of a night-club on the Kurfürstendamm. He worked long hours and the wages were just enough to pay for their room and food, and his share of the tips went on clothes and other necessities. After six months he was promoted to serving drinks in the bar, where his English was useful with American and English tourists.

The club's main business came from foreigners. Businessmen on a night out, looking for a girl, and long-term visitors like reporters and a sprinkling of writers and painters.

He had heard nothing about how the news of their escape had been received in Warsaw and Moscow because he had no contacts back there and had no intention of trying to find out.

It was two weeks before their first Christmas in Berlin and he had bought cakes and a bunch of flowers on the way home as an early treat. When he saw the police-car and the ambulance and the small crowd of people outside the building he knew at once that it was Anna. He didn't know what had happened but he knew it was her.

They had let him travel in the ambulance with her body. They had driven straight to the morgue and he had officially identified her body. And then at the police station there had been the questions. The detectives had been sympathetic and considerate. Almost as if they knew or guessed why she had been murdered. Garotting was generally confined to assassins and professional criminals. There were more questions about his son. Why did he think that he'd been taken rather than killed with his mother? What kind of people did he know who were so ruthless? Had he met any people at the club where he worked who might have had a grudge against him? But after a couple of hours they had let him go. It was obvious that they would not spend much time looking for the boy. They acted as if they were aware that he knew who had committed both crimes. The inquest would be held in two days' time.

He never went back to the rooms. For two days and nights he wandered the streets of Berlin like a lost soul.

Oblivious of his surroundings, his mind a turmoil of grief and hatred.

The inquest gave a verdict of murder by strangulation by a person or persons unknown. The coroner had commented on the fact that nothing appeared to have been stolen or even disturbed. But Josef has seen the small red star stamped on the inside of her wrist and for him it was not murder by a person or persons unknown. He knew all too well who had murdered her. Half demented, Josef had gone back to his job that night. There had been a great deal of sympathy for him. Staff and customers had seen the two small paragraphs in the evening paper.

Just on midnight he was serving a drink to a man he had seen several times before. He had been told that he was a journalist for one of the press agencies. When he had poured the double whisky the man looked at Josef's face, lifted his glass and said in Russian, 'To the dead, Josef. The living should remember it and learn the lesson.'

Josef felt the room spin and the man said quickly in English, 'My friend, I'm on your side. Make no mistake. I'll help you all I can.'

'Who are you, mister?'

The man half-smiled. 'Just call me Johnny.' He paused and said softly, 'I saw the red star before they took her downstairs.'

'You were there?'

'I was with the police inspector when they got the phone call.'

'What phone call? They never mentioned a phone call to me or at the inquest.'

'Somebody phoned in to the police HQ. They said she had been executed and gave the address. Then they just said – "The red flag will fly all over the world." They said it first in Russian and then in heavily accented German.'

'Why didn't the police mention it at the inquest?'

The man took a sip of his whisky. 'Who knows, Josef? Who knows?'

'How is it you speak Russian?'

The man shrugged but didn't reply.

'You're a reporter, yes?'

'A foreign correspondent. Much the same thing.'

'You knew what the red star meant?'

'Of course I did.' He paused. 'What are you going to do about it, my friend?'

Josef looked down at the bar-counter and wiped a damp patch with his cloth before he looked back at the man's face. 'I'm going to make those bastards pay a thousand times. I don't know how. But I'll do it if it takes the rest of my life.'

'Were you one of them way back?'

'Not way back. Six months ago I was one of them. I was a fool.'

'You're in good company, Josef. There are a lot of people being fooled by the thought of the brotherhood of man. They'll learn in due course.' He paused. 'I could help you do a lot to hurt them. Could we talk some time?'

'Prove to me that it'll hurt them and I'll talk all you want.'

'Are you staying at the same place?'

'No. I sleep here at nights.'

'How about three o'clock tomorrow afternoon.'

'OK.'

Almost every day for three weeks Johnny asked questions and listened. Josef was surprised at the reporter's interest in the people in the Cheka International Affairs section. Names and personal details, their families, their vices, favourite foods, their houses and their office responsibilities. It was five weeks after Anna's death when the journalist asked if Josef would like to go back to England.·

'They wouldn't let me back in.'

'I think it could be arranged if you went about it the right way. There's always people who are interested in what goes on in Moscow.'

Josef shrugged. 'They'd think I was a stooge sent in by the Cheka.'

'I know a lot of people in London. Would you like me to talk to them?'

'Yes. If you think it'd do any good. But don't get into trouble for my sake.'

'Look. Do you want to go back?'

'Yes.'

'Well, just leave it to me to see what I can do.'

The meeting with the British Consul had gone smoothly enough. After it had all been arranged the journalist asked for the Soviet passports that Josef and Anna had held, as souvenirs of their getting to know one another.

Josef disembarked from the boat at Newcastle, on January 22, 1924. He was twenty-two years old. There were two main items on the front page of the *Evening Chronicle* that night. Ramsay MacDonald had formed the first Labour Government that day, and Lenin had died in Moscow the previous day. Neither Josef, nor even the man who called himself Johnny, who spoke to him in the bar at the Railway Hotel later that evening, could have imagined the strange life that was starting for him that day.

2

The man who sometimes called himself Emil Goldfus and other times Martin Collins was nearly fifty when he signed the lease for the premises at 216 West 99th Street in New York. His birth certificate gave his age as fifty-three and no casual observer was likely to doubt it. He had the air of a European refugee academic. Rather old-fashioned but charming. Some of the people he met thought he looked rather sad. A sad man who put a brave face on life.

He banked a few hundred dollars a month at the 96th Street branch of the East River Savings Bank. And like any other customer there were small withdrawals from time to time. But unlike most other customers Emil Goldfus had similar accounts at banks all over the city. And at all of them, Emil Goldfus, retired photographer, was a respected client.

When he had first come to New York in 1950 he had spent his days studying the city. Riding the bus and subway routes, getting himself established locally with the neighbourhood shopkeepers, eating simple meals in the local cafeterias. He knew how long the express train took to get from his nearest station to Times Square and how to change lines for the Bronx or connect with Lexington Avenue. He never owned a car and seldom took taxis. There were two cinemas that he visited regularly. One he particularly favoured. Many people would have seen it as a mildly idyllic existence. Sitting on the park benches reading a paper, strolling along unfrequented streets, standing and staring sometimes at derelict buildings and weed-ridden plots of waste-land.

But there was no observer of the quiet unobtrusive oldish man.

There were two or three people who lived on East 71st Street who knew him. But they knew him as Milton, an Englishman.

Later in 1953 Goldfus moved to Brooklyn and rented studio space in a drab seven-storey building that flattered itself by having the name of the Ovington Building. The Ovington Building was on the outskirts of Brooklyn Heights and, in addition to the fifth-floor studio, Goldfus also took a room in a boarding house on Hicks Street.

It was a more expansive time in his life. He painted and sketched and slowly got to know a number of the artists who worked in the building. He was quite liked, the old-world charm and wry humour made him pleasant company. He made friends with several of the struggling artists who occupied the studios.

The couple he knew on East 71st Street were Mona and Morris Cohen, and he had been in touch with them from his first days in New York.

There were other people whom he met regularly on his strolls in the parks, or at the cinema. Some knew him as Emil Goldfus, others as Martin Collins or Milton. Some years earlier there were people who knew him as Andrew Kayotis.

He became an accepted and well-liked neighbour to several of the artists who shared the rooms in the building. His paintings were amateurish but he accepted criticism with good grace and seemed eager and determined to improve his painting skills. One of his neighbours even gave up a little of his time to teaching Emil Goldfus to play classical guitar. He joined in their late-night discussions and they came to the conclusion that Emil was no intellectual and marked him down as an elderly Socialist whose vaguely liberal views belonged more to the pre-war thirties than the late fifties.

Part Two

3

Despite its name, the Canadian township of Cobalt was better known for its silver mining, and in 1920 its population of just over a thousand was what you could expect in a boom town. Wildcat prospectors, surveyors, a handful of officials from Toronto and Ottawa, and the suppliers of goods and services that batten on such communities. Three hundred and thirty miles by rail from Toronto it was one of the richest silver deposits in the world.

Jack Emmanuel Lonsdale was a half-breed who found his life in Cobalt rewarding and congenial, and he reckoned he had made a good move when he married the immigrant Finnish girl. Their son Gordon was born four years later in 1924. But instead of cementing the marriage it marked the beginning of the end. Only a special kind of woman thrives in boom towns and even they see it as a place and a time to make your pile and then get out. The girl from Karelia saw no future for a family in the rough and tumble of Cobalt, and the couple slowly drifted apart.

The half-breed couldn't understand why the woman hated what to him seemed a veritable paradise of money, booze, and girls on the make. It was not so much a difference of opinions as a total inability to comprehend the woman's objections. When she eventually left, taking the boy with her, there was no rancour from the man. She wanted to go back to Karelia, to Finland, where she was born.

He gave her cash for the journey and enough for a few months' keep. He was neither angry nor hurt. It was just beyond his understanding. He never heard again from his wife or son and when, in 1940, the Soviet Union invaded Finland through Karelia he neither heard nor knew of the world's praise for the gallant Finns who fought back against overwhelming odds for over a month. So he never knew that his son was sixteen years old when he was killed or that his wife had died in a Soviet slave-labour camp a few years later. He had long forgotten them both and had no idea where Finland was. He had only the vaguest idea where Toronto was.

In the late spring of 1940 as the snows were beginning to melt in the forests of Karelia the special document unit of the NKVD had the unpleasant but routine job of checking the corpses that had been buried in the snow, and the log cabins, the homes that had been pounded by Soviet artillery. Documents of any kind were bundled up carefully and despatched to the NKVD's new Finnish headquarters in Helsinki for the central document unit to process and send on to Moscow.

4

The woman stood in the small sunlit kitchen watching the boy as he ate his Jell-o and and ice-cream. He was her sister's son and she had been pleased to have him. He was a bright, cheerful boy and had done well in his first year at the school. He was no trouble, he did as he was told and the Californian sunshine suited him. The chronic cough had disappeared after a couple of months.

When she reached for his empty plate she said, 'D'you want some more, boy?'

He shook his head. 'No more thank you, aunt.'

'I had a letter from your mother today. She sends you her love and told me to tell you that she's very pleased that you're doing so well at school.'

'Why isn't she write to me?'

'Why *doesn't* she write to me.'

'Why doesn't she write to me?'

'There are problems, boy. Government regulations and so on. It's not her wish, you can be sure of that.'

'What else she say?'

'She says there's still snow in Moscow and she's sending you photographs of the new apartment. Two rooms she says. She's very lucky.'

'Why doesn't she come and live here too?'

She walked into the small kitchen with the empty dishes. 'They wouldn't allow that.'

'Why do they allow it for me then?'

'I don't know, boy. All I know is the people in Moscow gave permission and here you are. What homework have you got?'

37

'Not much. Can I play with the Carter boys first?'
'Where?'
'In the park.'
'OK. But you've got to be back by seven.'
'Thanks. What does goose mean, aunt?'
'It's a bird. You had goose at Christmas.'
'Tom Carter said old man Field had goosed Jenny and he was reporting him to the sheriff.'
'That's a vulgar word, boy. Not a word you should be using nor young Carter neither.'
'But what's it mean?'
'I guess in that case it means grabbing a girl's backside. Now run on with you or you'll be back before you've started.'

It wasn't until 1938 and Konrad Molody was sixteen that he eventually went back to Moscow. It took him a few weeks to settle down. He missed the San Francisco sunshine and his friends, and Moscow seemed grim after the free and easy time in Berkeley with his aunt. But there were compensations. He spoke fluent and almost perfect English, and he had been given a place at Moscow University and that meant a sure career in some government department.

At the end of his first year at university he had been interviewed by two men. They were both Red Army officers. One a major, the other a lieutenant-colonel. They both spoke excellent English and they had talked English for most of the time, asking him about his five years in the United States. They obviously knew the United States better than he did but they talked as if he were the expert, especially on the details of everyday life. They were unlike any army officers he had talked with before. They were almost like Americans. Easy-going, amused and amusing, and no hint of using their rank. They seemed to know quite a lot about him and his background, but they gave no hint as to why they had talked with him.

When he saw one of them again, the colonel, the Germans were already into the Ukraine. Five hundred thousand

Russians had been killed or captured when they took Kiev. And now an army of a million men, seventy-seven German divisions under Field Marshal Bock, were heading up the open road to Moscow. Molody had been recruited into the Red Army and was driving an ammunition truck for an artillery battery. He had no uniform, just a band round his arm with a red star. A despatch rider had brought him a message to report back to the temporary headquarters in a bombed-out shop by the railway station at Volchonka-zil, one of the southern suburbs of Moscow.

Molody stood there in the flickering light of a paraffin lamp, his civilian clothes in tatters and his face pale and drawn with hunger and exhaustion.

'D'you remember me?'

'Yes, comrade Colonel.'

'Have you kept up your English?'

'Yes, Comrade.'

'Where are your parents?'

'My father died a long time ago. I don't know where my mother is. Our block was shelled but I heard that she survived.'

'I'm sending you on a training course. You'll be leaving Moscow tomorrow.' He looked at the youth's ragged figure. 'Have you got any other clothes?'

'No, Comrade Colonel.'

'You'd better come back with me. My car's outside.'

'I'll have to report to my officer.'

'Don't bother. He knows. Let's go before they start the night barrage.'

The colonel drove him to a villa way out of Moscow on the road to Vladimir. The rooms had been turned into offices and an officers' mess. He was given a meal and then told to be ready at six o'clock the next morning. He slept on a mattress on the floor of an empty room.

It was still dark at five o'clock but he was up and waiting. He was driven to an airstrip near Yaroslav. It took ten days by plane and trains to get to Sverdlovsk.

The training school was outside the city in a clearing

in the forest. Rows on rows of wooden huts behind a ten-foot stockade with an outer perimeter of barbed wire. It was to be his home for almost five years. The training he received as a future intelligence officer was thorough and comprehensive, and the extra year had been because he spoke fluent English. He attended lectures with four others on Canadian, US and British history, politics and armed forces. He himself gave several talks on his boyhood in California.

During all the remaining years of the Great Patriotic War he lived at the training school. Well fed, healthy and cut off from any aspect of the war. The war might not have existed for the students at the school. When he had completed the course Molody was made a captain in the MVD, the Soviet secret service. He was one of the youngest men ever to hold that rank.

In the aftermath of the war he was sent back to Moscow and in 1949 he married. She was a pretty girl named Galyusha, uncomplicated, amiable and affectionate. He was working in the directorate responsible for controlling and supporting MVD agents in overseas countries, and his own work was in the department responsible for espionage in the USA and Britain.

In 1953 he was sent to the MVD special training school at Gaczyna. He was away from his wife for six months. There were facilities for wives at Gaczyna but his applications for Galyusha to join him were refused. Moscow wanted him to get used to being away from his wife.

He was told things at Gaczyna about the MVD's operations in Britain that made him realise that even though Britain had been an important part of his control area there were many things that he hadn't been told before.

There were half a dozen pretty girls on the staff of the training school working as waitresses and housekeepers for the living quarters. Nobody said they were available. Nobody needed to. Molody had regular sex with two of them. He knew it would go down on his file because they wouldn't have been there if they weren't already trained

MVD operators. But they were there for sex as well as security and Molody liked pretty girls.

All the time he was at Gaczyna he was only allowed to listen to the BBC. News, entertainment and music. And his newspapers were the London nationals. Two days old. He lived in a single, isolated hut that was furnished with G-Plan furniture with a typically English lower-middle-class, suburban decor.

When he returned to Moscow he was given a month's leave and he and Galyusha went down to the sunshine of the Black Sea, using an MVD rest-house in Sochi as their base.

Galyusha was conscious of the benefits they got from her husband's privileged position. 'Hard' roubles, shopping privileges and a superior apartment in the centre of Moscow overlooking the river. She was allowed to go with him for the month he had in Leningrad. He spent long hours at the Red Navy base every day but she had been taken around the city by an Intourist girl who showed her the sights, and took her to good restaurants and cafés to eat. Galyusha was not much interested in galleries and museums but she loved the city itself. A few weeks after they went back to Moscow the doctor confirmed that she was pregnant.

Molody leaned over the rails of the boat where it lay at anchor in Kolsky Bay and looked across to the grey buildings on the dockside. There were nine months of winter in Murmansk and from November to mid-January there were no daylight hours. There were still old people in Murmansk who spoke the ancient local language, Saami. And in the Saami language Murmansk means 'the edge of the earth'. Already the town was shrouded in mist and it was still only July. He wondered why they had insisted that he travel by sea and he wondered too why he had to leave from Murmansk. Maybe they thought that if his last memories were of this grim town he wouldn't feel homesick. He wouldn't feel homesick anyway. He was a professional and what he was being sent to do was important. He was now a key agent and his new rank of major marked their recognition of his past

41

work and their confidence in him in his new role. It was 1954 and there had been the big purge in the MVD and he had not only survived but benefited. It was now the KGB and its responsibilities were even greater than before.

He turned and looked at the seamen who were battening down the last of the hatches. It was a grain transporter and there were only three other passengers.

The ship docked at Vancouver in the late afternoon and the Canadian excise rummage crew came straight on board. Molody made himself scarce and the crew-list for Immigration showed only three passengers. The three legitimate passengers had been cleared through Immigration in twenty minutes.

It was ten o'clock when Molody and one of the crew showed their shore passes to the security guards at the gate. They were warned that they had to be back by midnight. Molody had talked in broken English with a thick Russian accent and it had been all too easy. He handed over the pass he had used to the crewman and without a word he had walked off alone. A small, worn, cardboard attaché case in his hand.

Once he was away from the dock area he asked the way to the YMCA. They found him a bed for the night. He joined and stayed for another two weeks, and in that time he found himself an inexpensive one-room apartment and a job as a salesman in a radio shop.

In the next few weeks he used the genuine birth certificate that he had been given in Moscow and obtained what he most wanted, a genuine Canadian passport. He got a driving licence and a YMCA membership card and several other minor pieces of documentation that provided him with background material.

He changed jobs twice during the winter. Both moves got him increased pay. He had several girlfriends and his colleagues at work liked his easy-going ways. But behind the casual façade he worked hard, and the shop owner recognised that he was not only a good salesman but ambitious. He made several suggestions at the last shop that increased their turnover and profits and the owner seriously considered giving him a small stake in the business. But before he had formulated a suggestion the young man took a week's holiday and never came back.

Molody stood looking across towards Goat Island where the falls were split in two. The American Falls and Horseshoe Falls. Most residents on the American side of Niagara would reluctantly admit that the Canadian side was the pleasanter: commercialisation was not so all-pervading.

The two governments co-operated to make the formalities of crossing the border from one side to the other as easy as possible, and when Molody presented his Canadian birth certificate and his return bus ticket to Toronto he was passed through without query.

He didn't hurry, he joined the crowds and looked at the sights before he caught a bus to Buffalo and found lodgings for the night.

The following day he took a train to New York. He walked from the station to Fifth Avenue and the New York Public Library. He immediately recognised the girl at the enquiry desk from the description they had given him. When he asked her where he could find biographical material on John Dos Passos she turned to one of the huge reference books before she realised the significance of what he had said. Then she walked from behind the counter and he followed her to the far end of the library.

She turned to look at him, and said softly, 'Doris Hart,' and he said, 'Victor Seixus Junior.'

When he left he had the bundle of money and the key to the luggage locker at Grand Central. In the locker there was just the coded message.

He booked a room at the YMCA on West 34th Street and sat in the small room and decoded the message. He wondered what Alec would be like. He took a meal at a nearby automat and the evening paper headlined the news that Gromyko had taken over from Shepilov as Foreign Minister. It was February 15, 1957.

5

There were a few villas still standing near Łazienki Park. A dozen or so which had escaped both the German and the Russian onslaughts on Warsaw. Some people said that they had been deliberately preserved for the Russian officials to use when it was all over. But in the event they had been used by Polish officials of the new communist regime and one of them had been divided up into ten flats for junior staff who worked for the newly established foreign embassies.

Harry Houghton had one such flat. A small living room, a bedroom and kitchen and bathroom. Its furnishings were sparse and primitive but despite its size and starkness the minute apartment provided the best accommodation he had had in his life.

Born in Lincoln he had run away from home at sixteen and joined the Royal Navy. Obsequious and ingratiating, he had made little progress until war broke out. By the end of the war he had become a chief petty officer. A reasonably efficient clerk, he had legitimately used Admiralty regulations to get his officers their marginal extra service payments and had kept the messes supplied with black-market booze. Not liked, but tolerated for his ability to bend and manipulate service regulations on rations and supplies, he had never experienced a day's service in a battle zone until 1942 when he was assigned to merchant protection vessels on convoys to Malta and Russia.

He was demobilised in 1945 and joined the civil service as a clerk. For four years he served as an Admiralty clerk in the minor Navy port of Gosport near the big Royal Navy base at Portsmouth. At the end of four years he was assigned as clerk to the British naval attaché in Warsaw.

A line-shooter and a drunk, Harry Houghton was detested by the rest of the embassy staff. But it was in Warsaw that he spent the best time of his life.

Harry Houghton sat sprawled on the leather settee in the soft, pink light from the silk-shaded lamp which he had bought on the black market. With an unsteady hand he poured vodka into the deep glass and passed it to the girl on the settee beside him. Then he reached for the empty glass on the table and filled it slowly and carefully.

The girl was in her late twenties, dark-haired and attractive. Her face was flushed from drinking and as the Englishman lifted his glass to her she touched it with hers and said '*Na zdrowie.*' She laughed when he tried to respond in Polish.

'Is easier I say "cheers" for you, Harry.'

'Cheers, sweetheart. Did you sell the stuff OK?'

'Yes. No problems at all. They want all you can get.'

'What do they want?'

'Any drugs at all. But they pay most for penicillin and sulfa drugs.'

'How much will they pay?'

'Fifty US dollars for a tablet.'

'Jesus. That's good. How much have we got?'

She reached over for her worn leather handbag, took out a fat brown envelope and handed it to him.

'I haven't counted it yet.'

He looked at her, his eyes alert. 'Can you stay the night?'

She laughed and nodded. 'Is OK, Harry. If you want that I stay.'

He grinned. 'Let's count the cash first.'

For ten minutes he counted out the notes. There were $4,450 in used notes. He counted out a hundred and fifty and handed them to the girl.

'OK, Krissie?'

'You're very good to me, Harry.'

He smiled. 'It's your turn to be good to me now. Let's finish the bottle first.' He reached for the bottle and held it up. 'Bloody thing's empty.'

He stood up unsteadily and lurched across to the shelf of bottles and glasses and the framed photograph that showed him in uniform, grinning, with a glass of beer in his hand. He swore as the corkscrew split the cork and he shoved the cork into the bottle.

Back at the settee he poured another glass for each of them and drank his down and poured again. With his free hand he leaned over and pulled the girl to him, his mouth on hers, his hand pulling the strap of her dress from her shoulder.

Despite negative reports from the embassy and strongly critical reports from his immediate superior, Harry Houghton survived two years in Warsaw from 1949 to 1951 and in that time he had accumulated several thousand pounds in his bank account in England. He had lived an extraordinary life in the post-war ruins of Warsaw. Kristina had introduced him to some of the richest people in Warsaw. The black-market operators and the collaborators with the Soviet occupation controllers. Notorious for his crude behaviour at embassy social events, he was frequently seen drunk in broad daylight on the city streets.

After he was back in England he still sent a few cheap cosmetics to Kristina, but without the diplomatic bag there was no possibility of sending more antibiotics. Despite the fact that he was sent home for chronic drunkenness he was given a security clearance and a job at the Underwater Weapons Establishment at Portland naval base, a secret installation employing over 20,000 people and concerned only with submarine and anti-submarine research. When Harry Houghton joined the establishment, HMS *Dreadnought*, the Royal Navy's first atomic submarine, was being fitted out with its American atomic plant. But Portland's main task was to improve NATO's underwater defence programme in detecting and destroying enemy submarines. He joined the base in 1951, and lived in a village just outside Portland itself with his wife Peggy.

6

Molody stood looking across the street at the hotel. Somehow it didn't look like the photographs he had been shown. But it was the right name and the right address: Hotel Latham E. 28th Street. He couldn't remember what made it seem different and he walked across the road, into the hotel lobby and took the elevator to the seventh floor. And then walked up the stairs to the eighth.

For a moment he hesitated as he looked at the number on the door. 839. That was the room number all right. And the name on the card was the name he expected – Martin Collins. He looked both ways up the corridor and then pressed the bell.

The man who opened the door was thin-faced and balding and he recognised him straightaway. He had been shown photographs of the man in Moscow. The man recognised him too, nodded impassively and stood aside to let him in.

For a moment, after the door was closed, they stood looking at each other. They had never met before or communicated in any way, but they were Russians in a strange, dangerous country and instinctively their arms went round each other and they kissed cheeks like old friends meeting.

Collins looked at the younger man, his observant eyes taking in the details of his face, his hands still on the young man's shoulders.

'How long are you staying in New York, my friend?'

'As long as necessary, as short as possible.'

'There are a few people I want you to meet while you are here. They could be useful to you some day if things go wrong over here.'

'Are you expecting trouble?'

'No.' Collins smiled. 'But after ten years you bear it in mind. Have you eaten today?'

'Yes, comrade, but I'd appreciate a drink.'

Collins would have preferred vodka but he always kept to whisky, Jamiesons, to go with his Irish name. He poured them generous glasses before he sat down.

Molody looked around the large almost empty room. A single bed, a heavy, wooden artist's easel alongside a small table and a stool and canvases leaning against the walls.

Molody looked back at his companion. 'Does it make you a living?'

Collins frowned. 'It *is* my living, comrade, I'm an artist. Anything else I forget. My name is Collins, my father was Irish and I'm a New Yorker.' He shrugged. 'You have to be convinced. If I don't believe it why should others believe it? It's the most important thing you can remember.'

'You mean having a good cover?'

'No. I mean never having a cover.' He waved his hand at the room. 'This is not cover. This is me. My life. It's real. Neither you nor anybody else could convince me otherwise. This is reality. If there is anything else then it is a small secret in my mind. Like a married man with a mistress or a man who likes being whipped. Anything else is a small secret vice in the back of my mind. You must work out for yourself what you want to be and then *be* it. Every minute of every day.' He put down his glass. 'What do you want to be?' He smiled. 'Fulfil your dreams my friend.'

Molody laughed. 'A millionaire.'

'So be it, comrade, make money, be a businessman. It's no more difficult than being an artist. Do it as if that is the only thing you care about. Don't pretend. Be a tycoon.'

'Who are the people you want me to meet?'

'Do you know Jack Sobell?'

'I don't know him. I've seen his file.'

'And?'

'Moscow instructed me to avoid him. He's under suspicion.'

'So I understand. But he had two people working for him before he fell out of favour. A married couple. The Cohens. First-class agents. Experienced, disciplined and committed. The man was a teacher here in New York. Had an excellent record, but Moscow moved them from Sobell's control to another ring that was eventually exposed. When the Rosenbergs were betrayed I managed to warn the Cohens in time for them to go underground. They are intending to go to England. I've kept them back so that you could meet them.'

'Would Moscow approve?'

Collins smiled. 'You are independent now, comrade. It is up to you to decide. All that Moscow wants from you is results. How you get them is up to you. Who you use is up to you. You cut the cord with the Centre when you boarded the ship in Murmansk.'

'When can I meet them?'

Collins looked at his watch. 'In an hour. You know the zoo in Central Park?'

'No. But I can find it.'

'Fine.'

Collins gave him a password, pointed out the meeting point on a large-scale map and instructions on how he should be contacted again if the chalk mark was on the wall of the toilet at the cinema. He was to check for the mark every day.

7

Sir Peter Clark's office was the only deliberate reminder in the building of their connection with the mandarins of Whitehall and the Foreign Office. Panelled and finished in the highest Civil Service good taste, it acknowledged that the Director-General of MI6 was still a servant of the Foreign Secretary despite his privilege of direct contact with the Prime Minister if he felt it necessary. And 'necessary' usually meant when some MP was heading for something worse than a domestic scandal, something that could affect national security. The old-fashioned and rather ornate office was neither typical of the man's character nor a sign of self-importance but an overt symbol of the D-G's awareness of his political masters.

Once a top Civil Servant himself in the Ministry of Defence when it was called more frankly the War Office, Sir Peter knew where the levers of Whitehall lay and how to operate them. Tall and lean, he looked like something out of P.G. Wodehouse but it was totally deceptive. A double-first at Balliol, a blue for boxing and a brain that had won him the respect of both the soldiers and the politicians.

He looked across at his deputy, Hugh Morton, one of the organisation's old China hands who had survived the swings and roundabouts of MI6's turbulent fortunes because he was a wise assessor of both men and situations. Sir Peter pointed at the file that lay on his desk between them.

'What did you think of that little lot?'

Morton shrugged. 'Looks more like a job for Five and Special Branch to me.'

'Why? Because Maguire-Barton's an MP?'

'Yes.' He had smiled. 'And a government MP to boot.'

'Maybe that's why Five have suggested that we handle it.'

'Did they give any reason why they suggested that?'

'Yes. They see Grushko, the Russian, as the one who really matters. Not Maguire-Barton. They think he's just a stooge.'

'I'd agree that Grushko is the one who really matters but I don't see Maguire-Barton as a stooge. He's too sly and too ambitious for that.'

'What's his rôle then?'

'Who knows? Agent of influence maybe.'

'Influence in what area?'

'We'll know more when we've looked them over. He's got influence in the House. Cultivates journalists. Appears on chat shows and TV. He's got plenty of opportunities for pushing the Soviet view either openly or covertly.'

'Who'll you get to handle this?'

'Shapiro.'

Sir Peter pursed his lips. 'Is it important enough for Shapiro to handle?'

Morton smiled. 'You don't like him do you?'

Sir Peter shrugged. 'Like, maybe not. Admire, yes. He knows the Soviets inside out, but when an MP's involved I wonder if somebody less obsessed might not be more suitable.' Sir Peter paused. 'But I leave it to you.'

'Any comments on our submission for an increased budget?'

'Plenty. Most of them unfavourable. The opposition hate our guts and there are plenty on the government side who'd like to cut us down to size. The only consolation I ever have at the budget meetings is that they give Five even more stick than they give us.'

'Why do you think this is?'

'It's a combination of two things in my opinion. It's popular with the media to denigrate our intelligence services and on the other hand they're scared of what we know about them.' He laughed softly. 'Of what they think we know about them. When I hear them talking on the budget committee I can hear the skeletons rattling in their cupboards.' He shrugged and stood up slowly. 'Thank God it's only once a year. I don't mind the criticisms but the sheer hypocrisy angers me.' He paused. 'Keep me in touch from time to time about Maguire-Barton.'

'Is it urgent?'

'I don't know, Hughie. We won't know that until Shapiro and his chaps have found out a bit more.'

Harris, sitting at his desk, wore a faded blue denim shirt and twill slacks to mark the fact that it was a Saturday morning. Chapman wore a light-weight grey suit and a dark blue cravat instead of a tie. There was some sort of emblem or coat of arms on the cravat. Hand-embroidered.

'Tell me what you've been doing since you came into SIS.'

'All the way back?'

Harris nodded. 'It's not all that way back. But yes.'

'I did the basic three-month training course and then six months at St Antony's on the history of the Soviet Union and the organisation of the KGB and the GRU. I got Beta-minus on both. Then I worked for Lowrey for a few months on surveillance.'

'What kind of surveillance?'

'The Oxford Group and Jehovah's Witnesses.'

'On your own or with Lowrey?'

'Both. About half and half.'

'Go on.'

'I did surveillance as part of a team on the Czech Embassy and then I did solo on two suspected KGB safe-houses.'

'Which ones?'

'The small one in Highgate and one in Kensington.'

'Who did you report to?'

'Joe Shapiro.'

'Tell me about Joe Shapiro. What kind of man do you think he is?'

'I didn't really get to know him. He's a bit high up for me.'

'You must have got some sort of an impression. What was it?'

Chapman hesitated. 'He won't be told what I say, will he?'

Harris raised his eyebrows in obvious disapproval of the question. 'No. And I doubt that he'd be interested anyway.'

'I found him a very strange man. Absolutely dedicated. Any crumb of information about the KGB or the Soviet Union was pounced on as if it might be vitally important. He wanted to know every detail. What they wore. Did they look pleased or unhappy. Had they had their hair cut since I last saw them. If they ate out he expected to know everything they ate.' Chapman smiled uncertainly. 'He even said that he wondered if lip-reading ought not to be part of our training.' Chapman paused, hesitating. Then he went on. 'He made me feel that he was very like a KGB man himself. More than just dedicated . . . fanatical.'

Harris's face was non-committal. 'Go on.'

'I guess that's about it. I admire him. His knowledge and his expertise. But . . . you know, when he was de-briefing me I felt that he got a kick out of knowing every little detail. I'd talked to men who he knew all about. He didn't seem much concerned that I'd made a cock-up of the surveillance or that I'd blown my cover-story.' He hesitated. 'I found him a bit odd.'

'Did they brief you on what you might be doing with me?'

'No. They said you'd tell me.'

'Tell me about yourself.'

Chapman smiled. 'I'm sure you've checked my "P" file.'

'Maybe. But you tell me.'

'I'm thirty next October. I went to Eton and Oxford. Played a bit of tennis. Messed about in France and Germany for a couple of years. Doing odd jobs. Tour agency's courier and that sort of thing.' He shrugged. 'I guess that's about it.'

'Tell me about your father.'

Chapman looked uneasy for the first time. 'He runs an engineering outfit in Stafford. He's pretty good at it.'

'Why don't you work for him?'

Chapman smiled. Rather wanly. 'He never asked me to.'

'Why not? Your brother works for him.'

Chapman looked away towards the window and when he looked back at Harris he said quietly, 'He doesn't think much of me.'

'Why not?'

'I'm not sure. I think he thinks I'm rather feckless, and not commercially minded.'

'What did he say when you told him you were in SIS?'

Chapman laughed softly. 'He wasn't impressed. Said it was a bunch of academics and queers.'

'Sounds quite a charmer.'

'He had to fight his way up the ladder. He's not so bad.'

Harris reached for the two files. 'I've got them to free an office for you. Number 431, two doors down the corridor. Read these and come and see me at three.'

When Chapman had left, Harris sat thinking about what Chapman had said. His assessment of Joe Shapiro had been very perceptive for someone who couldn't know anything about his background. Not that he knew all that much himself.

And Chapman hadn't mentioned that his father had a knighthood and he hadn't mentioned that he was Chairman of Carlson Engineering who employed about eight thousand people and was the biggest firm of its kind in the north Midlands. Maybe it wasn't modesty, maybe he took it for granted that everyone knew that he was the son of Sir Arthur Chapman, who paused grim-faced for the TV cameras as he walked into some Ministry or harangued some meeting of the CBI on how the country should be run. His donations to the Liberal Party were as acceptable as his membership was frequently an embarrassment. Nobody could understand why he had joined the party when he was so obviously a right-wing Tory in word and deed. But he added a touch of reality to party conferences and committees, and at election times canvassers discovered that his views were shared by many old-fashioned working people. They too thought that taxes were too high and that blacks should go home unless they played for Arsenal or Lancashire County Cricket Club.

There was one other thing that Chapman had said that registered with Harris, but he didn't recall it when he was going over their conversation in his mind. But subconsciously it had made him change his attitude to taking on Chapman. He'd at least give him a fair run for his money.

8

A lot of people thought that Shapiro looked remarkably like Spencer Tracy in *Guess Who's Coming to Dinner*. His face had the same topography and his hair was white and luxuriant. His eyes too had that same speculative, disbelieving, wary look. Only a handful of people knew what his responsibilities were, and any questions on the subject were treated with evasion or outright condemnation of the questioner for indulging in idle curiosity. But everyone knew that he had been with MI6 for longer than any serving officer could remember. Joe Shapiro was part of the fabric of the organisation. They knew he had been an officer in MI6 well before World War II. And they knew that he had a hand in almost all operations concerning the KGB. But that was all. There were rumours of an unhappy marriage that surfaced from time to time but there was virtually nothing known of his domestic life.

He was talking on the phone when Harris knocked and came in and Shapiro pointed to one of the chairs in front of his desk. When Shapiro finished talking he hung up and turned to look at Harris.

'I've told Morton that if we're to do this job properly we're going to need at least four or five more bodies.'

'Did he agree?'

Shapiro shrugged. 'He agreed. But that doesn't mean we'll get 'em. I gather you've taken on young Chapman.'

'Yes. There wasn't a great deal of choice.'

'Any suggestions of how to tackle this thing?'

'I thought maybe I should cover Grushko and let Chapman cover Maguire-Barton. Until we get more people.'

'There's not much in either file that's of any real use. Gossip column stuff about Maguire-Barton and four or five days of random surveillance of Grushko. But they've met on a dozen or more occasions in the last twelve months. Not always in this country. Two so-called parliamentary visits to Prague, one to Sofia. A trade fair in Dresden and a few sponsored jaunts to East Berlin. Ostensibly exchanges of views on East-West relations and general arms reductions. The usual crap.'

'How often do you want me to report?'

'Every day. A written summary every week.'

'Can I use your secretary?'

'You're out of date, laddie. I haven't had a secretary for two years. Use the pool and if there's any delay I'll deal with it. You just let me know.'

Three days after seeing Shapiro, Harris met Chapman at Victoria Station and they walked together to Harris's rooms.

'Tell me what you've got.'

'I've divided my time between Maguire-Barton and Grushko. But I haven't got much.'

'Tell me about Grushko. I'll be taking him over myself and you can concentrate on Maguire-Barton.'

'Grushko's got a flat off Kensington High Street in Adam and Eve Mews. It's over a garage where an antique dealer keeps some of his stock. He's got a special lock on the door and a rather primitive light-cell and an old-fashioned pressure alarm under the mat inside the door. It's quite a pleasant flat and a woman from the embassy cleans it every other day. A good collection of classical cassettes and a Jap hi-fi. A lot of books. A few Russian but mainly English and American. Novels, poetry, social history. I've made a list.'

'Any correspondence or files?'

'No. Absolutely nothing. The postman hasn't made a

delivery there since he took over six months ago. His mail must go to the embassy. None of them have much mail even at the Press Centre. And that's all official stuff from UK sources. Invitations, press releases. That sort of stuff. But there is one thing. He's got a bird he sees regularly. A real doll. Looks Russian or Italian. Very dark, flashing eyes and rather sultry.'

'Who is she?'

'I haven't found out anything about her except that she doesn't live permanently in London. She generally spends the night with Grushko when they meet and she takes the Cardiff train home but I don't know where she gets off. Once or twice she's stayed at a flat in Hammersmith after meeting Grushko. I'm checking on whose flat it is.'

'Is she anything more than a girlfriend?'

'I think she is. I'm not sure.'

'Why do you think that?'

'They're obviously fond of one another. But they look like conspirators.' He laughed. 'They seem to talk almost too much and too earnestly for just lovers.'

'What about Maguire-Barton?'

'He's got a pad in Pimlico. A conversion. Three bedrooms. Quite swish. And it's paid for by a public relations company. Lobbyists. It's pretty exhausting following him, he's a real busy bee. Goes to everything he's invited to. Especially embassy parties. Mainly eastern bloc ones but to others as well. And what's even more interesting is that our friend Grushko is nearly always at the communist receptions at the same time. But they never leave together. And . . .' he paused, smiling, '. . . the most interesting thing is that Grushko's girlfriend has been escorted by Maguire-Barton on two occasions. Once to the Italian Embassy and once to the Dutch Embassy. Grushko wasn't there on either occasion.'

'Anything else?'

'Maguire-Barton has two or three girls he sees regularly. All-night jobs. Sometimes his place, sometimes theirs.

Seems to be a lavish spender. I asked for permission to check his bank account but Painter says he needs more grounds before he could authorise it.'

'Have you checked over Maguire-Barton's file in Archives?'

'It doesn't go back very far. They've not been checking him for long, and before the surveillance started there's very little if anything of interest to us.'

On the tenth day Chapman followed Maguire-Barton's taxi to the Embankment on the south side of the river and walked behind him as the MP strolled past County Hall towards the Festival Hall.

Chapman hung back as Maguire-Barton walked into the Festival Hall and across to the cafeteria. He saw him standing with a tray in the short queue for tea and then Chapman saw Grushko sitting at one of the window tables alone.

Grushko and Maguire-Barton sat at separate tables but after ten minutes Grushko stood up, walked to Maguire-Barton's table and bent over for a light for his cigarette. Smiling his thanks the Russian picked up the folded newspaper from the table beside Maguire-Barton's arm and walked back to his seat. Maguire-Barton left five minutes later and Chapman followed him back to the flat in Pimlico. It was the first time that they had established a positive and covert connection between the KGB man and the MP. Harris confirmed later that Grushko had met his dark-haired girlfriend at the Golden Egg in Leicester Square. They had gone to the Zoo and then back to his Kensington flat. He left alone at eight o'clock the next morning and later the girl had taken the Cardiff train.

9

The cabin on the SS *America* was small, with two berths, one over the other, and two small lockers for clothes and hand luggage. But Molody had slipped the steward ten dollars and he had got the cabin to himself. As he sat on the lower berth he wondered why Collins had ordered him to leave the United States within forty-eight hours. The orders came from Moscow and he was to go to London and be prepared to stay there indefinitely. It didn't seem like a routine posting. He had been doing a good job for Collins in the United States but Collins had seemed tense and apprehensive. He had been given the London address of the Cohens who had apparently already moved to England. But Molody wasn't a man who indulged in doubts and introspection.

For the first two days he had been mildly seasick but by the third day he had recovered. He spent a lot of his time playing cards with some of the stewards and it was from them he learned about the Overseas Club which provided cheap accommodation in London. He learned too about the various rackets the crewmen ran to augment their earnings, and he realised that there were going to be even more opportunities for earning quick easy money in London than he had had in Canada and New York.

He found the crewmen impressed by his story of his wealthy Canadian father with the huge estate in Vancouver, and he regaled them with stories of how, despite the money his father gave him, he had worked as a cook in a labour camp, as a gold prospector, a long-haul truck driver and a gas-station attendant. By the time the ship docked at Southampton he had added to his legend a nagging wife who he had walked out on. It seemed to go down well and bit by bit he had fabricated a past that explained and fitted his present life and character.

At the Royal Overseas League off St James's Street he only added to his story that he had been given a Canadian government grant to study Chinese at London University's School of Oriental and African Studies. A far-seeing government was anticipating a relaxation of contacts that could lead to trade with Red China.

Two weeks later he had a job as a second-hand car salesman in Clapham. He was successful from the first day and although he was only paid commission he was earning reasonable money. But not enough money to justify the flat he took in the White House, a residential hotel in Regent's Park. But the legend of the wealthy father covered that, and his fellows at the car showrooms were impressed by his constant flow of anecdotes about his life in Canada. He found that, like Collins had said, he already believed his own story. He could bring himself to raging anger at the indignities heaped on him by his imaginary wife and could bring tears to his own eyes as he reluctantly revealed the unhappiness of his childhood. Neglected by his frivolous mother, his wealthy father too often away abroad on business trips.

The advertisement in the *Evening Standard* offered the opportunity for investors to get into the vending machine business and Molody had telephoned the next morning.

He'd spent an hour with the two men talking about their proposition. They wanted £500 down and he'd be given a small territory to sell machines in. To offices, canteens and clubs. But there was no chance of him having a stake in the business. He had offered up to £1,000 for a five per cent shareholding but they'd refused. Molody was impressed by the two Jaguars in the tatty yard outside. And he was impressed by their refusal of an offer that valued their business at £20,000. There was only one room and the

62

two lock-up garages that housed the vending machines. He got on well with both men, they were amiable rogues, as talkative and confident as he was and they finally gave him the telephone number of a firm that handled juke-boxes.

The man with the juke-boxes was an altogether different sort of man. Big and rough, he was obviously not interested in Molody's amiable chat. If Molody paid a hundred-pound deposit in cash on each machine he could have up to five. Take it or leave it. There were no exclusive territories and no sales leads. It was all up to him. He paid the deposit on five machines and stood watching as the man counted every note.

In six days of tramping the streets of Clapham Molody had placed seven juke-boxes, and by the end of two months had a regular income of over two hundred pounds a week in cash. An income on which he would pay no tax and was therefore worth more than double what it netted him.

In his journeys he heard of a syndicate in another district selling and renting one-armed bandits that was looking for an additional partner. They were in Peckham, and Molody invested several thousand pounds and became a substantial shareholder and a director.

From the office he set up in Rye Lane Molody worked from early morning until late at night. Gradually his partners let him take over and he became managing director. He was then planning how to make extra profits by setting up a plant to manufacture machines for them to sell. He had already started exporting machines. There was only one condition he laid down and that was that he was to have all weekends free.

The girls who phoned and called for him at the small offices were much admired by his colleagues and when he came in on Mondays looking tired he made no protest when they made their schoolboy jokes about why he always wanted his weekends free.

10

Alongside Portland is the small seaside town of Weymouth. Its harbour has provided safe anchorage for invading Saxons, Romans and Normans. But when it became a favourite resort of George III it became better known for its sandy beach and old-world peace.

The Old Elm Tree public house in Weymouth had Harry Houghton as one of its regulars. Night after night he regaled the other regulars with stories of his war-time exploits. They listened with amusement, exchanging winks, because they were well aware that his tales were often self-contradictory, manning naval guns in Mediterranean convoys at the same time that he had been twenty below zero on an ice-gripped convoy to Murmansk. But with his mottled, red-veined face and his pointed nose he was harmless enough. He was a bullshitter but he livened up the bar-room chat. He was always there promptly at opening time and he seldom left before the bar closed. It was well known that he didn't get on with his wife.

It was in May 1958 when his wife contacted the probation service in Bournemouth and arranged an interview. Probation officers are reluctant to hear complaints about third parties who have not been put under their control by the courts, and it often turns out that their informants are more in need of help than the alleged offenders. But listening is part of their official therapy.

Mrs Houghton's interviewer was a cautious man and he listened without comment to her litany of her husband's drunkenness, neglect, unfaithfulness, and his determination to get his own back on the Admiralty who had ruined his career prospects. It was an old, old story that had been retailed with variations on the theme hundreds of times in every social service office in the kingdom and when all this seemed to rouse no indignation Mrs Houghton played her trump card. She claimed that her husband regularly brought home classified documents from the naval bases. When even that brought no response she gave up.

The probation officer thought vaguely of passing the information to naval intelligence but decided against it. The woman was almost certainly lying, from spite against her husband. And if he passed on such information and it turned out to be a pack of lies God knows what repercussions there could be. Actions for defamation, libel and all the rest of it. Anyway, none of her problems concerned the probation service. It was the Marriage Guidance Council she needed or Special Branch. Or, more likely, a psychiatrist.

Ethel Elizabeth Gee was forty-six, and a temporary clerk at the Portland navy base. With small features and a clear complexion she looked younger than her years but very plain. Expecting little or nothing from life, she was surprised and flattered when Harry Houghton started paying court to her. Even when it had matured, their relationship was far short of a romance but in some odd way it satisfied them both. The meek timid woman saw the man as a protector; not quite a hero, but a man who had seen something of the world. He spent money freely, took her on trips to London, and everywhere he went he seemed to get to know people easily and quickly. And for the man, he had a sympathetic listener and a woman who didn't despise him, who mended his clothes and cared about whether he had eaten enough.

'Call for you, Harry.'
   'Who is it?'
   'Don't know, mate. A fella – he said it was personal.'

65

Harry Houghton reached across the desk for the receiver and put it to his ear as he scribbled a note on a file.

'Houghton. Who is it?'

'I've got news of Kristina for you, Mr Houghton.' The voice was soft and had a slight foreign accent.

'Who are you?'

'A friend of Kristina. She asked me to talk to you.'

'Is she coming over then?'

'Maybe we should meet and I can give you her news.'

'Where do you want to meet?'

'I suggest you come up to London and we meet outside Drury Lane theatre on Saturday next. About twelve o'clock mid-day.'

'How shall I recognise you?'

'I'll recognise you, Harry. Don't worry.'

And the caller hung up. Houghton reached for his mug of tea. It was cold but he sipped it slowly as he thought about the call. Kristina had always said that she wanted to get out of Poland and come to England. It would complicate things but by God it would be worth it to have a girl like that to show off to his friends.

He found it hard to concentrate on his work for the next two days. And in the evenings when he and Ethel were decorating the empty cottage that he had bought in Portland he wondered how she'd take it when the time came. She was a dignified woman so she'd probably not make a fuss. And that bitch Peggy would have finished divorcing him and it would be one in the eye for her when she heard he'd got a pretty young girl as his new wife.

Houghton stood in front of the theatre looking at the front page of the early edition of the *Evening Standard*. There was a picture of the President of Italy in London on a State visit. He looked up from the paper. There were plenty of people about but nobody who seemed to be looking for someone. He turned to the stop-press. Chelsea were playing at home. He'd just be able to

66

make it to Stamford Bridge if the chap on the phone didn't turn up.

And then a hand touched his arm. 'Glad to meet you, Harry.'

The man was tall. Younger than he had expected.

'Glad to meet you too.'

'Where can we have a coffee and talk?'

'There's a place round the corner.'

'You lead the way, my friend.'

When the waitress had brought the tea and coffee and the buttered toast Houghton couldn't wait any longer.

'How is she? How's Krissie?'

'She's got problems, Harry. She needs your help.'

'I'm nothing to do with the embassy now you know.'

'I know that, comrade.'

'What's the problem anyway?'

'She's got problems with the police. They know about the drugs and the black market. It's a very serious offence you know in Poland.'

'Who says she did such things?'

The man smiled. 'They've got statements from the buyers. Dates. Places. And she's confessed, so they have a clear court case.'

'How can I do anything?'

'Well, Harry, she feels she's only in this mess because she wanted to help you. She thinks that the police might be more lenient if you co-operated.'

'Co-operated. How?'

'There are things the authorities would like to know. If you helped them I'm sure things would go better for Kristina.'

'There's nothing I can tell them that Kris couldn't tell them. I just brought the stuff over.'

'I'm not thinking of that business, Harry, I'm thinking about your present work. There are small bits of information that we should like to know.'

Houghton looked at the man's face. 'You mean tell you things about Portland?'

'Yes.'

'I couldn't do that. I'm not allowed to. You ought to know that.'

The man shrugged. 'It could be very bad for you if you don't, Harry. Bad for your lady-friend too.'

'You mean they'd . . .'

The man held up his hand. 'Let's not talk about that. We both know the facts of life. And nothing will happen if you co-operate.'

'I'll think about it.'

The man shook his head, dismissively. 'In future when we are to meet you will receive a brochure in the mail offering you a Hoover vacuum cleaner. When you receive this you will phone this number and ask for Andrew.' He pushed a scrap of paper across the table. 'When you phone you say your name and you will be given a time and date. Nothing more. No talk. At the time and on the day given you go to a public house called the Toby Jug. You already know it, don't you.'

Houghton nodded. 'Yes.'

'Anything else, my friend?'

'What the hell do I get out of all this?'

The man reached inside his jacket for his wallet and below the table he counted out eight one pound notes, folded them over and then passed them over the table to Houghton. 'That's for your expenses, Harry.'

The man stood up, put a pound note on the table alongside the bill, gave Houghton a brief cold smile and left.

It was beginning to snow as Houghton walked into Covent Garden, and he walked down into the Strand and across to Charing Cross Station and changed trains at Waterloo.

The train was almost empty and he sat alone in the second-class carriage thinking about the man. They were bluffing of course. They could play their games in Russia and Poland but not in England. He would ignore the whole thing. Put it out of his mind and forget it. He picked up his copy of *Reveille* and leafed through, glancing at the

68

pictures. At no time did it occur to him to report the matter to the police or the security officer at Portland. It was just a try-on that hadn't worked.

And as the days went by he *did* forget about the meeting and the threats. And he was all the more shocked when a month later he got a brochure through the post offering a special deal on Hoover vacuum cleaners. He was shocked but not scared. He hadn't enough imagination to be scared. But he phoned the number the following day and he was given a time and a date.

The man came into the Toby Jug five minutes after Houghton sat down at one of the tables. He wasted no time after he had ordered two beers.

'What have you brought?'

Houghton passed him half a dozen back copies of the *Hampshire Telegraph and Post*. He pointed to one of the back pages, to a regular column headed 'Naval and Dockyard Notes'.

'That's all very useful stuff.'

The man read the column that consisted of nothing more than routine published information on ship movements and naval promotions and postings. He pushed the newspaper to one side and turned in his seat to look at Houghton.

'Is this meant to be some sort of joke?'

Houghton shrugged. 'That's all I can do for you, mate.'

'Maybe you don't believe my warning about what could happen to you and your woman.'

'You can't do anything in this country. You'd never get away with it.'

The man looked at him with half-closed eyes as he spoke. 'I'm going to give you one more chance, comrade. If you don't respond sensibly you're going to be in very deep trouble.'

And without further words the man pushed aside the table and walked out of the pub.

For the first time Harry Houghton wondered if they really would dare to try something. For a couple of days

69

he thought about it from time to time. But he was getting ready to move his belongings from the repository and the trailer he had moved into while he and Ethel decorated the cottage. It had taken months but it would be ready for Christmas and there was a lot to sort out now that he was on his own.

But when another Hoover brochure arrived in the post the first week in December he decided to ignore it. When in doubt do nothing was Harry Houghton's motto.

11

The small shop in a side-street just off the Strand had shelves from floor to ceiling with row on row of books. Books were piled high on half a dozen tables and books were stacked on shelves up the stairs to the small second storey. In the small untidy inner office a glass-fronted bookcase held the really expensive volumes.

They were books of all kinds except fiction and the majority were about the Americas. The United States, Canada, South America and the Polar Regions. History, geography, economics, politics, flora and fauna, the arts, anything related to the Americas.

When the bell on the street door clanged a small white-haired man came down the rickety stairs and walked over to the man who had come in.

'Don't let me disturb you if you want to browse. You're very welcome to look around but if I can help you . . .'

'Maybe you can. Have you ever heard of a guy named Moore, a poet?'

'You must mean Clement C. Moore, died about 1860 or thereabouts.'

'That's pretty good. Yes, he's the guy. He had a book published called *Saint Nicholas*, something like that.'

'Ah yes. Actually *A Visit from Saint Nicholas*.'

'That's the one. You got it by any chance?'

'No. I could get you a copy maybe, if you're not in a hurry.'

'How long would it take?'

'Oh, that's very hard to say. Months rather than weeks, I'm afraid. Especially if you wanted the original edition.'

'Yep. That's what I wanted. Well maybe I'll leave you my card. I'm at the US Embassy. I'll give you a call in a few months' time.'

'I'll see what I can do, sir.'

When the customer had left the white-haired man went back up to his small office and sat looking at the visiting card. The American was the naval attaché at the US Embassy. He reached for the telephone, hesitated, then slid the card into the drawer of his desk. He was fifty, a spry, healthy-looking man with a ready smile and already well-respected in London's antiquarian book world. It was known that he was a New Zealander and only just established, but he knew his subject and had a reputation for fair dealing. He didn't deal in the areas that most dealers covered, he was a genuine specialist and he passed on leads to other booksellers for a small commission. And even apart from business he was a likeable man. He didn't talk about his past but that was understandable. He was a Jew and he had been in Europe before he became a refugee to New Zealand. People assumed that he had a background of persecution and concentration camps as many others did who were now in London. Nobody wanted to open old wounds, neither his nor theirs.

He and his wife lived in a typical London suburb in a modest bungalow. 45 Cranley Drive, Ruislip, was quite small. Mock Tudor with white-washed walls and fake beams with a small front garden and a drive up to the garage. His wife, Helen, was forty-seven, also white-haired and with alert eyes that were always on the edge of a smile. Obviously well-educated and capable she looked a very compatible wife for her bookseller husband.

The bookshop didn't open on Saturdays. It wasn't worth it, and apart from that he needed his weekends free.

He was up in the attic when his wife called up to him.

'The phone, Peter. For you.'

'Who is it?'

'Our friend.'

72

He clambered down the ladder, brushing the dust from his clothes and in the hall he picked up the phone. It was only a short conversation and then he walked into the kitchen.

'He'll be here at mid-day. I'd better finish the attic. I'll need the vacuum cleaner.'

The three of them ate together. *Borsch* and *pirozhki* followed by lemon sorbet. When the woman left the two men together they got straight down to business.

'When can you take the radio?'

'Now if you want.'

'Where are you putting it?'

'Under the kitchen floor.'

'Isn't that risky?'

'No. It's the last place anyone would look.'

'And the aerial?'

'I've already fitted one in the attic.'

'Don't forget to give me that American's visiting card. That could be very useful.'

He smiled, patting his jacket pocket. 'I haven't forgotten it.'

12

There had been a Hipcress farming on the Romney Marshes long before Napoleon contemplated invasion, and one of the early Hipcresses had helped dig out the channel for the Military Canal. They were none of them good farmers although they were financially quite successful. They had a hunger for land that outran their husbandry. All farmers complain about the weather and the crops but Albert Hipcress didn't complain. He seethed silently with anger against the government, the tax office, the National Farmers' Union and neighbours with more than his five hundred acres.

Hipcress was a bachelor of forty-five, and with his unprepossessing appearance and his country bumpkin manners seemed likely to remain one. But he assumed that every woman on the marshes, single or otherwise, saw him as a prime target because of his five hundred acres. His farming was simple and primitive. Potatoes, beans, and sheep. His lambing record was poor, but his feed costs were minimal.

The farmhouse itself was a pleasant, rambling old house alongside two disused oasts, and beyond the oasts were two large metal-clad barns. The shepherd's cottage was a hundred yards away, barely visible from the farmhouse itself.

Albert Hipcress sat in the farm kitchen next to the Rayburn solid-fuel cooker, reading a week-old copy of the *Kent Messenger*. He wore a pair of old felt slippers and a pair of shiny blue serge trousers held up by a pair of army braces. He looked up at the old clock on the mantelpiece. There was half an hour yet. He used the tool to lift the hotplate, spat into the fire and wiped his mouth on the back of his hand. He walked through to his tiny office that had once been a larder and switched on the light. Taking a bunch of keys from his trouser pocket he unlocked the bottom drawer in the ancient roll-topped desk, took out a blue folder and turned over the pages until he came to the balance sheet. He had not only read it many times before in the past month but he could have recited the figures blindfolded. The farm itself was valued at £672,000. The stock was written down to £7,000 and the plant and machinery at £24,320. Albert Hipcress used contractors to avoid capital expenditure. But the last figure was the one that pleased him most. Cash at bank. £943 on current account and £34,000 on deposit. The scattered cottages that he owned were not included in the farm accounts.

He walked through to the bedroom. The light at the side of the bed was already on, the bottle of whisky and the two glasses were on the cast-iron mantelpiece over the gas-fire. The corner of the sheets was turned down neatly on the bed. And then he saw the lights of the car as it went over the hump-backed bridge across the feeder to the canal. He was downstairs, waiting at the back door as it swept in to draw up between the oasts where nobody could see it. He heard her high heels as she hurried across the concrete yard. Then he saw her and she was the one he'd asked for.

'Hello, Mr H. How are you?'

He nodded. 'Not bad. How are you?'

The girl laughed softly. 'Rarin' to go, honey.'

Upstairs he sat on the edge of the bed watching as she took off her sweater, chatting to him, her firm young breasts swinging and bouncing as she struggled with the zip of her skirt. And then she was naked, standing smiling at him as he stared at her body.

'There you are, Mr H. That's what you've been waiting for all the week isn't it?'

75

It was seven o'clock the next morning when she left the farmhouse and hurried over to the cottage.

The Romney Marshes are not dairy country, its bleakness and its terrain can only support sheep, and the Romney Marsh sheep were bred to withstand the biting winds and the soggy marshland. On the marshes shepherds had always been known as 'lookers' and on the Hipcress farm the 'looker's' cottage was almost hidden from the farmhouse by a mild slope of the ground and a small copse of beech trees.

There had been no 'looker' on the Hipcress farm for the last twenty years and the cottage had stood empty for most of the time. Albert Hipcress had often wondered if there wasn't some way he could make some cash out of the 'looker's' cottage. He spoke to the estate agents in Rye and a few weeks later they had sent a man to see him. The estate agents suggested that he could possibly get seven to ten pounds a week rent for the cottage provided it was tidied up a bit.

Hipcress took an instant dislike to the man the agents sent to look at the cottage. He was a city man, smiling, confident and condescending. But when Hipcress said ten pounds a week the man had accepted. When they looked over the cottage together Hipcress said that it was up to a tenant to put it in order and bear the cost. The man had agreed to this too and Hipcress took him back to the farmhouse and wrote out a rental agreement from a tattered copy of *Every Man His Own Lawyer*. He asked for three months' rent in advance and was amazed when the man not only agreed but paid in cash.

He had watched the 'looker's' cottage being cleared out and furnished and wondered why a man would go to so much trouble when he only used the place at weekends and once or twice a month on weekdays just for the night. Slowly he changed his opinion of the man who was always so amiable and who frequently brought him a few bottles of beer. Two or three times on Saturday nights the man

76

walked over to the farmhouse and chatted with him in the kitchen. He couldn't remember how they'd got on to the subject of girls and sex. From the way the man talked he obviously expected that Hipcress had a girl now and again. He seemed amazed when Hipcress said that he'd never been able to find a girl to oblige him that way.

The following weekend the man had shown him photographs of two girls and asked him which he liked best. Albert Hipcress studied the two photographs as carefully as if he were judging the Miss World contest and finally pointed at the picture of the young blonde. The man smiled. 'You've got a good eye for a girl, Albert. She's a real goer that one.' He looked at the farmer, 'She's a friend of mine. How about I fix for her to come down with me in the week and give you a nice time?' Albert Hipcress was torn between the embarrassment of letting an outsider know his innermost thoughts and his desire for the girl. 'Just try her, Albert. I'd like to know what you think of her.' Albert Hipcress put up only token resistance and it was obvious that he was eager to take advantage of the man's offer.

Twice a month the girl had been brought down to the farmhouse. It cost Hipcress nothing and he was an enthusiastic and willing learner. When a visit was due, his mind as he worked around the farm was obsessed by thoughts of what they would do on the ramshackle bed in his room upstairs. His tenant never asked him if he liked the sessions with the girl and he never mentioned them himself. But he wondered how the man persuaded the girl to do it. He guessed it must be money. It wasn't the man's looks. His face had not even one good feature and his sallow complexion was especially unattractive. His eyes were always half-closed as if he was watching carefully; his nose was shapeless and his small mouth was mean. When Hipcress had asked him what he did he'd said he was a businessman

77

but he didn't say what business he was in. Most men would have wondered why, if it was money that made it possible, a stranger should spend money on him. But Albert Hipcress never wondered what the man's motive might be.

13

When the reception clerk phoned through to Joe Kimber he listened with no great interest. At least once a week some nutter came to the US Embassy in Paris, offering the innermost secrets of the Politburo or his services to the CIA.

'Can he hear you talking to me now?'

'No. I've shoved him in the annexe.'

'What's he look like?'

'Pretty rough. Tensed up and tanked up.'

'Did he speak French or English?'

'English. But real bad English. A heavy accent.'

'Tell me again what he said?'

'He said he was an officer in the KGB. He'd just come from his assignment in the US and he wants to defect.'

Kimber sighed. 'OK. I'd better have a look at him. Tell one of the guards to bring him in.' He cleared everything off his desk except the two telephones and drew the curtains over the map on the wall. He didn't get up from his desk when the Marine brought in the visitor. He pointed to the single chair.

'Sit down, Mister . . . I didn't get your name.'

The man shrugged. 'Is Maki or Hayhanen – whichever you like.'

The American smiled. 'Which one do you like?'

'My real name is Hayhanen but I use Maki name in New York.'

'Tell me about New York.'

'I work there for KGB.'

'So what are you doing in Paris?'

'I was recalled by Moscow. I don't wish to go. I am afraid.'

'Why are you afraid?'

'I think they discipline me. Punish me.'

'Why should they do that?'

'I don't know. I think the man in New York gives bad report on me.'

'Which man is that?'

'Is two men. Sivrin at United Nations and an older man named Mark. He never liked me from the beginning.'

'Why not?'

'He was old-fashioned. No friendliness. Just orders. All the time he criticise everything I do.'

'And who is this Mark fellow?'

'He is top illegal in United States.'

'Where did you have meetings with him?'

'All over. Central Park; RKO Keith's Theatre in Flushing, a cinema; Riverside Park; a place on Bergen Street in Newark.' He paused and shrugged. 'Many places.'

'What nationality are you?'

'Russian-Finnish.'

'You speak Russian?'

'Of course.'

'What about Sivrin?'

'I work at first for Sivrin. Then Mark.'

'Where did you meet Sivrin?'

'Was not much meeting – was mainly drops.'

'Where were the drops?'

'A hole in the wall in Jerome Avenue in the Bronx, a bridge over a path in Central Park and a lamp-post in Fort Tryon Park.'

'What was your address in New York?'

'We've got a cottage at Peekskill.'

'You mean Peekskill up the Hudson?'

'Yes.'

'Who's we?'

'I don't understand?'

'You said *we've* got a cottage. Who else is involved?'

'Just my wife. She lives there with me.'

'You mean she's still living there?'

'Of course.'

Kimber sat looking at his visitor, uncertain how to deal with him. He needed to check on at least some of the items in his story before he decided what to do with him. It was such a ragbag of a story but it had that faint smell of truth. There was one fact he could check on easily. And it was worth a call to the States.

Kimber looked across the desk. 'I'm going to get one of our people to take you to have a meal downstairs. He'll bring you back to me when you've finished. OK?'

Hayhanen nodded and stood up. Reaching into his jacket pocket he took out a Finnish five-mark coin and, as Kimber watched, the man prised the coin open with the nail of his thumb. The coin was hollowed out to take a single-frame negative from a Minox camera.

Half an hour later, after Kimber had phoned New York for a check on Sivrin and the cottage in Peekskill, it was Washington who came back to him. Seats had been booked on the night-flight from Paris for him and his visitor. He was not to interrogate him further himself. Just deliver him safely at Idlewild. He was to stay behind on the plane with Hayhanen until all the other passengers had left and a CIA deep interrogation team would come on board and take over.

When they arrived at Idlewild Kimber was amazed at the group that poured into the empty aircraft. Six or seven top men and Allan Dulles himself in the private room in the terminal building. It seemed that Hayhanen was the break they had been looking for for the last four years. He was congratulated as if it were some skill on his part that had pulled in the KGB man. There was apparently no doubt in their minds that Hayhanen really *was* genuinely KGB.

*

Two hours after his arrival in New York Hayhanen was officially handed over to the FBI and four Special Agents had interrogated him through the night to mid-afternoon. By that time he had signed a document giving his permission for the house in Peekskill to be searched.

They had to use Russian-speaking agents in the following days because Hayhanen's poor English became unintelligible under pressure. Apart from the language problem it became obvious that Hayhanen had a very disturbed personality as well as being a heavy drinker. Questioning Hanna his wife and several local tradesmen who knew him was like cleaning an old painting. As a layer of paint or varnish came off a different picture was revealed, and another and another. Hayhanen's life had been a strange, wild nightmare of drunken wife-beating, bizarre outbursts of public violence and then the secret life controlled by the man called Mark.

The interrogators gradually realised why Moscow had recalled him. Apart from keeping the appointments with his controller, Hayhanen had been totally indifferent to his mission. Using the money he was paid for his own purposes, unscrupulous in his demands for more funds and, as far as they could tell, never carrying out even the minor tasks that he had been ordered to undertake. But what they got from him that really mattered was the description of Mark, the places where they met and the various addresses in New York where he lived or appeared to live. As often happened when a man really hates another, Hayhanen could describe Mark in great detail.

It was the studio in the Ovington Building that they were able to identify most accurately despite the vague, rambling description, and a twenty-four-hour surveillance of the building was mounted by the FBI even before the interrogation of Hayhanen was completed. The interrogation team were going back into his recruitment and training in the Soviet Union but Hayhanen was slowly disintegrating, becoming fearful of KGB retribution for what he had done. Nervous and excitable, he refused to sign statements and insisted that even if they were able to trace the man named Mark, he would not appear personally in court as a witness to Mark's activities.

His description of Mark had portrayed an elderly man, bald with a fringe of grey hair, a narrow face with a prominent nose and a receding chin; he thought that maybe Mark was Jewish. And always the dark straw hat with the broad white band around it.

14

Bert Harris stirred his coffee slowly as he watched the two men at the table near the service counter. One of the men was Grigor Grushko and he had no idea who the other man was. It was the second time they had met in the last two weeks. The first time they had met at a pub, the Bricklayer's Arms near Victoria Station, and this time they were in the cafeteria on the main concourse at Euston Station.

They were talking earnestly, with Grushko tapping his finger on the table as if to emphasise some point. They weren't quarrelling but it looked as if they were disagreeing about something. Ten minutes later Grushko stood up, standing for a moment, still speaking as if he was trying to convince the other man of something.

Harris looked at his watch. It was four-thirty and he decided, for no particular reason, to stay with the second man. But he watched as Grushko walked across the concourse and down the steps to the underground taxi rank.

Ten minutes later the second man looked around the cafeteria slowly, and Harris was sure then that the man had had anti-surveillance training. It had been done too methodically, despite the casualness. The man stood up, patted his jacket pockets as if to check that something was there, and then he walked across to the bookstall and bought a copy of the *Evening Standard*. He turned it sideways to look at the stop-press column on the back page, folded it slowly and strolled across to the exit to Euston Road. He stood outside looking at the passing traffic. Harris watched him from just inside the station.

When the man walked to the line of taxis Harris was close behind him. After the man closed the door of the taxi Harris let one taxi go and took the second. He flashed his ID card at the driver and pointed to the taxi he wanted followed.

They were held up by the lights in Regent Street but the target taxi had turned into Beak Street and was heading for Golden Square where it stopped by the Dormeuil building and the man got out. Harris waited in the taxi for a few moments watching the man walk across the gardens towards Berwick Street. Then he paid off the cabbie and followed the man into Brewer Street. In Old Compton Street the man turned into an open doorway leading to a flight of stairs. A handwritten postcard tacked to the door merely said, 'Sunshine Escort Agency.'

Harris crossed the street and looked up at the dusty windows of the agency above the newspaper shop and couldn't for the moment think of anything positive he could do. So he waited. Fifteen minutes later the man came out with a young girl. He guessed she was about eighteen. She was very pretty. He followed them both to Cambridge Circus where the man waved down a taxi. It had circled the roundabout before there was another empty taxi and he'd told the driver to go down Charing Cross Road and they caught up with the other taxi as it turned into Charing Cross Station.

He heard the man ask for two tickets to Folkestone and the clerk said that a train was due to leave in twelve minutes which had given Harris time to buy a ticket and phone through to Shapiro for some assistance. No assistance was available.

Just over an hour later the man and the girl got off the train at Ashford in Kent. Harris walked ahead of them and took the first taxi, telling the driver to wait. It was nearly five minutes later when the man and the girl came out of the station and Harris breathed a sigh of relief as they got into a taxi themselves. He had to use his ID card again but the driver co-operated well. Harris asked him to check with the taxi company's despatcher where the white Granada was going. The reply was that it was going to Stone-cum-Ebony to Cooper's Farm. The driver said he'd been there himself a month before, with a fellow and a girl. It was old man Hipcress's farm. When Harris asked him to describe the male passenger he knew that it was the same man. The driver also volunteered that when he had done the trip he'd been told to pick them both up at the farm the following morning in time to catch the 9.15 from Ashford to London.

The white Granada was already heading back for Ashford as they turned into the lane that led past the farm. The driver slowed and stopped, winding down his window to talk to his colleague. He was going straight home. He'd got to pick up his fare at 8.15 the next morning. Harris paid off his driver a hundred yards past the farmhouse and asked him where was the nearest public telephone box. It was half a mile away at the bend in the lane, where it joined the main road to Rye.

The farmhouse was reached by a gravel drive, there was one light downstairs and one light upstairs in the gable end and Harris stood in the darkness, listening and watching. Apart from the distant bleating of sheep and the sound of water running in the ditches everywhere was silent. When his eyes were accustomed to the darkness he made his way cautiously up the drive.

When he was about twenty yards from the farmhouse he saw that the gravel drive gave way to a cinder track rutted from farm vehicles. As his eyes followed the ruts he saw the lights in the 'looker's' cottage by the trees. There were two cars parked by the cottage. A Mini and a Rover 90.

Harris waited for ten minutes before he approached the farmhouse. As he edged his way along the wall towards the lighted window he could see that the curtains were open and when he looked inside he saw that there was nobody in the room. It was a farmhouse kitchen. Quarry-tiled floor, a solid fuel cooker, big oak table and old-fashioned chairs. The sink and cupboards were modern and cheap. From the overhead beams the old hooks for carcasses still hung down. On one of them was an oil-lamp, its glass shade cracked and dusty.

The 'looker's' cottage was not so easy. There were lights on all over but the curtains had been drawn. There was a small gap in the curtains at one end of the downstairs window but the view of the inside of the room was blocked by a man standing with his back to the window. He could hear voices but not the words. He had a feeling that they were talking in a foreign language. The rhythms were not English.

Then the man moved away and he saw that it was the man he had been following. He was offering sandwiches to a white-haired man, a man in his fifties, and a woman who was a little younger. They were talking animatedly, shrugging and shaking their heads. Then they laughed at something the man had said.

Harris made his way cautiously back to the lane. He had no idea where it led but he followed it to the telephone kiosk and phoned the duty officer. Fifteen minutes later a police car picked him up and drove him back to Ashford Station.

The Vice Squad from West End Central applied some discreet pressure to the agency's proprietor. The girl's name was Judy Manners, she was twenty-two and she had a room in Islington. The client was a Mr Gordon. He always paid cash and they had no address for him. He paid £80 and the girl got half.

A plain-clothes policewoman from the Vice Squad picked up the girl and brought her in to West End Central for Harris to interview. The three of them sat around the table in the stark interview room. The girl defiant but obviously scared.

'What are you charging me with?'

'Nobody's charging you with anything – yet,' the police-woman said.

'So why am I here?'

'The gentleman wants to talk to you.'

The girl glanced at Harris. 'Go on then – talk.'

'You went with a man a few days ago to a farmhouse in Kent. Yes?'

'So what?'

'What was the name of the man who took you there?'

'You'd better ask the agency, mate.'

'They said his name was Mr Gordon. Is that correct as far as you know?'

'Yeah.'

'How many times have you been to the farm with him?'

'Three times – maybe four – I don't remember.'

'Always with Mr Gordon?'

'Yes.'

'And what happens at the farm?'

'You know bloody well what happens.'

'I want you to tell me.'

'It's none of your business.'

'I can make it my business if you'd like it that way.' The girl turned to look at the policewoman.

'You can't touch me. Everything I do is legal.'

'So tell the gentleman what you do.'

The girl turned her head to look at Harris. She shrugged. 'OK. He screws me.'

'Who? Mr Gordon?'

'No. For Christ's sake. The old man, Hipcress or whatever his name is.'

'What about Mr Gordon? What does he do?'

'God knows. He goes off to the cottage. He meets his friends – I go over there in the morning and Mr Gordon takes me back to London.'

'Is it straight sex with the old man?'

'More or less. He plays around for a bit but there's nothing out of the ordinary.'

'Have you ever had sex with Mr Gordon?'

88

'No.'

'Does Mr Gordon talk about himself at all?'

'He chats. He obviously fancies himself with girls but he never makes a pass.'

'What does he chat about?'

'Nothing special. Football sometimes – I think he said that he's a Portsmouth supporter. I think his friends come from Portsmouth or it could be Plymouth. I don't remember which. He's obviously got plenty of money.'

'What does he do?'

She laughed. 'At first he used to give me this spiel about being in entertainment. He sounded off like he was running the Palladium or at least a club.' She laughed again. 'It turns out that he flogs one-armed bandits.' She shrugged. 'He obviously makes a lot of dough but it sure ain't showbusiness.'

'Have you got any idea where he lives?'

'No.' She hesitated. 'It's near Regent's Park I know that – and it's posh. He showed me a photo of his main room. Some sort of party for his friends.'

'Is he English?'

'No – he's Canadian.'

'Did he seem to be on good terms with the farmer?'

She shrugged. 'He thinks he is. But the old man told me on the quiet that he didn't really like him. Thought he was too full of his own importance.'

'What do you think of him?'

'I never made me mind up about him. He wasn't mean or anything like that. But there was something odd about him. I don't know what it was. A bit scary.'

'What did you think about the farmer?'

She laughed. 'He's all right – just a dirty old man.'

Harris stood up. 'You've been very helpful, Miss Manners. We much appreciate it. I'd like you not to talk about our conversation with anybody. Especially Mr Gordon. Is that understood?'

'Yes.' She nodded. 'Is that all?'

'Yes. Can we give you a lift somewhere?'

'You're not doing the agency for anything?'

Harris smiled. 'Of course not. Not so long as you don't talk with *anybody* about being here today. I'm sure the agency is a very well-run business concern.'

'Well,' she said, 'you know where to come if you want me.'

A routine check on the two cars at the cottage had been inconclusive. The Mini belonged to a middle-aged spinster in Weymouth and the Rover 90 was registered in the name of Peter John Kroger at an address in one of the outer London suburbs. A check with the local police showed that Peter Kroger was a dealer in antiquarian books. Married, the couple lived a quiet middle-class life and were regarded well by their neighbours. A check on the bookshop indicated that the man was considered an expert in his field by other booksellers and the business was modestly successful. A contrived inspection of the house by Chapman posing as a Ratings Assessment Officer from the local council proved negative. It was a typical suburban house and there were no signs of anything suspicious.

Harris applied for a specialist search team to check the cottage at the farm but it took two weeks before it was available and a pattern of the farmer's daily movements had been established. The only opportunity seemed to be his regular visit to Ashford Market on Wednesdays, and the search team were assembled and briefed the evening before. They estimated that they would need three hours for a Class A search but would only need half an hour for a routine check. Harris decided on a Class A and the team moved in when the radio link confirmed that the farmer's Landrover had gone through Appledore village.

A Class A search was based on the assumption that the target site was operated by a trained agent and where security precautions might have been taken either to prevent search or merely to reveal that a search had taken place. The team made their entry from an upstairs window and neither the front nor rear door of the cottage were opened. They were the most likely places for check-traps to have been laid.

Before the search team started, the photographer, with a Polaroid camera, photographed every wall and feature of every room. And as the search started he recorded the layout of every drawer as it was opened, and nothing on any surface was moved until its position had been recorded.

The technicians applied stethoscopes and thermocouples to the walls and floors of every room to check for cavities, and a two-man team checked all the inside and outside dimensions of the whole building room by room. There were two bedrooms upstairs, one living room below, a good-sized kitchen and what had once been a pantry. As soon as they saw the two elaborate locks on the pantry door they guessed that the search was going to be worthwhile.

Everything was neatly laid out. A small pile of one-time pads, a Minox camera, a photo-copying stand, a standard KGB micro-dot reader, photographic paper and chemicals, plastic trays, a Durst enlarger, and an almost new ICOM transceiver, and a label with transmission and reception times and frequencies pasted on its case. It was the first of the missing jig-saw pieces, and there was only one snag. There wasn't a single clue as to who Mr Gordon was. But they were justified now in extending the surveillance on the cottage as well as on Mr Gordon and Grushko.

15

The FBI's surveillance team's first sighting of Mark was on May 23. He paid a brief visit to the studio late in the evening and with the aid of a radio-link a team of two agents followed him when he left. Along Fulton Street to Clinton through to Montague and down to the Borough Hall subway station. He was followed to the City Hall stop where he got off, walking north on Broadway to the corner of Chambers Street, where he took a bus and got off at 27th Street. Up Fifth Avenue the FBI man followed as his quarry walked the block to 28th Street and turned the corner. But when Special Agent McDonald reached the corner of 28th Street and Fifth Avenue there was no sign of his man.

It was three weeks before they saw him again, and once more it was late at night when the lights went on in Studio 505 in the Ovington Building. It was ten minutes before midnight when he left and although the route was different this time the journey still ended at 28th Street, and this time they watched him enter the Hotel Latham. It was just past midnight on June 13 and the report of the sighting went back to FBI headquarters. The hotel register showed that the man Hayhanen called Mark had booked in under the name of Emil Goldfus. The FBI notified the New York director of the Immigration and Naturalization Service, and from there a report on Hayhanen and the surveillance operation was passed to the Internal Security Division of the US Attorney's office.

What could seem to outsiders as an exercise in passing the buck was, in fact, the reverse. When espionage is involved and the suspect is not a citizen, either born or naturalised, Federal Law requires the legal procedures to be followed meticulously. If the accused comes to trial on charges of espionage the evidence has to be concrete and conclusive or any experienced defence lawyer can reduce the prosecution case to one where nothing more than deportation can be the outcome. When prosecuting foreigners or illegal immigrants every step of the legal process has to be observed. If, as now seemed possible, Goldfus was an illegal immigrant, he would have to be brought to justice by the INS, but that would not give powers to the FBI or the CIA to use the arrest to obtain evidence of espionage.

The head of the Internal Security Services decided that without Hayhanen giving evidence in public, in court, they had too little evidence to bring a charge of espionage. He sent two of his attorneys to talk to the only witness – Hayhanen.

For two days and nights they talked, argued, pressured and persuaded but Hayhanen adamantly and angrily refused to go beyond just talking. He said he was afraid of reprisals by the KGB against his family in the Soviet Union. They also realised that he was genuinely afraid that the long arm of the KGB could reach out for him, even in the United States. He would go on answering their questions but he would never testify in court.

Nielson turned in his chair to look at the CIA man standing at the end of his desk.

'Nowak, I warn you. If you people – and the FBI – don't get your asses out of this operation this guy may never come to trial. We won't even be able to hold him for more than a week.'

'This is crazy – this guy is . . .'

Nielson cut him short. 'I don't care whether it's crazy or not. We have a warrant and a show cause order drawn up in Washington and that's enough for us to pull him in. But if you people try to ride in on the back of these, nothing you uncover or find will have any legal standing in a charge of espionage and will never – I repeat, never – stand up in court. Without Hayhanen giving evidence in court and subject to cross-examination you haven't got a leg to stand on. Even with Hayhanen testifying in court you may not make it anyway.'

'For Chrissake, man, this guy is . . .'

Nielson stood up waving his hand dismissively in front of him.

'Don't shout at me, Paul. The law is the law. I don't make it, I just administer it.'

Nowak shrugged. 'Can I ask you something off the record?'

Nielson relaxed and said quietly, 'OK. Go ahead.'

'Is somebody protecting this bastard behind the scenes?'

Nielson looked surprised. 'I've seen nothing that would make me think that. Why do you ask?'

'We know this guy has been the principal KGB man in the whole of the USA. For years. He's been running a network of agents very efficiently from what we've learned. Why has he never been picked up before? And why is everybody so anxious to protect him now?'

Nielson shrugged. 'The first question I can't answer, Paul. The United States is a big place. It's easy to disappear if you want to. About people protecting him – there's no one protecting him in my department. It's you people we're protecting. Warning you that you'll come to grief if you don't stick to the rules.' He paused. 'It's as simple as that.'

'If we risk it – what then?'

'You'd be gambling. If you didn't get a confession from him you'd be put through the mincer by the defence attorneys.' He shook his head. 'I wouldn't want to see that happen.'

16

On June 21, 1957, despite the warnings of legal compli-
cations, there were a dozen FBI agents in or near to the
Hotel Latham. Two officers from the INS were waiting in
Room 841.

Just after 7 a.m. an FBI agent knocked on the door of
Room 839, and a few moments later the man who called
himself Martin Collins and Emil Goldfus, naked and still
half-asleep, had opened the door, and as they walked into
the room the two FBI men had showed their identification
cards to him. Then a third man joined the two agents and
stood by the open door.

Nobody was sure who had actually authorised the
operation in that form but they knew very well what
their instructions were. They could question the suspect
for up to half an hour. They could tell him that he was
suspected of espionage but not charge him. He was to be
given every encouragement to 'co-operate' and that meant
indicating that he was willing to give them details of his
activities and maybe offer to 'come over'. The possibility
of him becoming a double-agent was the prize, but any
kind of co-operation could be considered a victory. If
neither outcome seemed possible he was to be arrested by
the two INS agents under section 242 of the Immigration
and Nationality Act.

By the time the half-hour was up he had given his
name as Martin Collins and admitted the obvious – that
he resided at the Hotel Latham. And nothing more. He
seemed subdued but not scared and he remained silent to
all other questions.

When INS agent Boyle read out the warrant for arrest it was in the name of Martin Collins a.k.a. Emil Goldfus. He had been given the routine caution that he was entitled to consult a lawyer and had a constitutional right to remain silent.

At INS headquarters he was fingerprinted, photographed and searched. And for hours he was questioned, the INS agents asking him again and again to co-operate. But he consistently refused.

Back at the Hotel Latham, the FBI search team was checking the room thoroughly. They had been amazed that a professional spy should have left around so much incriminating evidence of his trade. And there was still the studio to be searched if they could get a judge to sign a search warrant.

A few days later three affidavits were presented to a district judge in Brooklyn and after checking the statements he had agreed that sufficient cause had been shown to allow the studio search to take place. The warrant listed specific items but included wording that covered almost anything they might find that could be connected with espionage. The last sentence of the warrant seemed innocuous enough, but it marked a major change in the official attitude to the case. It said – '. . . which material is fitted and intended to be used in furtherance of a conspiracy to violate the provisions of 18 USC 793, 794 and 951.'

The charge of being an 'illegal alien' carried a maximum penalty of deportation. The conspiracy charge could lead to a death sentence.

It looked as if someone on the government side had decided to go for broke, because making that change involved considerable risks for the prosecution. It was feared that the switch could be challenged in court on grounds that it was unconstitutional. In addition, the conspiracy charge entitled Goldfus to a hearing without delay, and without the evidence of Hayhanen in court whatever they found, in itself,

96

would definitely not be considered as proving a conspiracy.

By the end of the day two things had happened that made it look as if the gamble had succeeded. Between the hotel room and the studio they had amassed a wide selection of espionage material. One-time pads, hollowed-out nails, nuts, bolts and pencils, cryptic messages, a Hallicrafter short-wave radio, bank books and microfilms. And in mid-afternoon Reino Hayhanen had agreed to testify in court. June 28, 1957, suddenly seemed a very good day.

17

They were only half a dozen people in the Warsaw LOT office on Ulica Warynskiego. He gave the girl five złotys for the airport bus ticket. Five minutes later they boarded the bus and the man took a window seat. He was tall and well-built, in his mid-thirties, his black hair cut very short. His right hand guarded the worn black leather briefcase on the seat beside him.

With the darkness came the rain, sweeping across the fields and the blocks of flats that lined the road to the airport. He guessed it would be snow by the time they got to Moscow.

At Okecie airport there was time for a coffee. He bought a copy of *Pravda* and settled down at the table, lighting a cigarette, his arm resting protectively across the black briefcase on the table. It was half an hour before he heard the airline announcement.

'Uprzejmie prosimy pasażerów odlatujących rejsem 207 do Moskwy o zgłoszenie się do wyjścia numer 3.'

He stood up and joined the queue at Gate 3. He could see the plane on the feeder runway, an old Antonov AN24. It looked as if it would be a crowded flight. It was generally full on the Friday evening flight to Moscow. Solemn-looking Soviets going back to spend the weekend with their families, hoping that their pretty Polish girl-friends were not being too blatantly unfaithful while they were away. And, of course, one or two upper-echelon Polish *apparatchiki* heading for a few sybaritic days at the Central Committee Hotel, or even a guest-apartment in Sivtsev Vrazhek and a walletful of privilege roubles for purchases at the discreet place on Granovsky Street that went under the name of 'The Building of Passes' but was really the treasure-trove of the *nachaltsvo*, the Kremlin élite.

They had been airborne for nearly half an hour when the stewardess announced that owing to technical difficulties on the ground the flight was being diverted and would not be landing at Moscow's main airport, Sheremetyevo, but at Vnukovo II. Vnukovo was the almost secret airport used only by top Soviet officials and never the general public. Kretski wondered what difficulties could have caused such an extraordinary diversion. He checked his watch. They were already ten minutes overdue. There seemed to be some consternation among the other passengers, and a man whose face he recognised as a senior Russian official had beckoned to the stewardess. And when she leaned over to listen to him Kretski could hear that his voice was raised in anger as he pointed at his watch. The stewardess nodded and left and a few minutes later the co-pilot came back to talk to the man, obviously anxious to placate him.

There was a long wait on the ground before they disembarked, and as Kretski walked across the tarmac the snow was swirling and already thick on the ground.

As he gave up his boarding card at the desk two men walked out from behind the metal screen. He didn't know them but he knew instantly that they were KGB. The older man said in Russian, 'Mr Kretski, I'd like you to come to my office.'

'What's the problem, comrade?'

The man smiled. 'No problem at all.' He nodded towards the white-walled corridor and the smaller man led the way, opening a door at the far end. And Kretski noticed the security locks and the bars on the windows.

The older man pointed to a plain wooden chair by the small bare table and drew up a similar chair on the other side. Kretski was aware that the second man was leaning back against the door, lighting a cigar.

'My name is Pomerenko, Comrade Kretski. Would you prefer to talk in Russian or Polish?'

Kretski shrugged. 'It's up to you.'

'You are Jan Kretski, yes?'

'Correct.'

'Deputy chief liaison officer between KGB and Polish Z-1?'

'That's right.'

'And you must know why you are here?'

'Not until you tell me, comrade.'

'Maybe it would be easier for you if we spoke English.'

'I can speak English if you prefer it.'

Pomerenko smiled. 'I am KGB, Comrade Colonel. Directorate Four. You have been under surveillance for two months and two days. And you are now under arrest.'

'On what charges, may I ask?'

Pomerenko leaned back slowly, his hand reaching into an inside pocket, taking out an envelope, looking at it for a moment before he pulled out a photograph and laid it, facing Kretski on the table.

'Tell me, comrade – who is that?'

It was a grainy black-and-white photograph, obviously blown up from the original, but he knew all right who it was. He wondered who had taken it, and when. He could just make out the archway at the back of Horse Guards Parade. He made sure that his hand didn't shake as he put the photograph back on the table.

'Who is it, Comrade Kretski?' Pomerenko said softly.

'You tell me.'

Pomerenko pointed. 'The name is on the back – look at it.'

As Kretski leaned forward for the photograph Pomerenko clamped his big paw down on Kretski's hand.

'You looked very pleased with yourself that day in the sunshine, didn't you?'

Pomerenko released Kretski's hand and as he turned over the photograph Kretski leaned forward. There was a typed label on the back. Just two lines in Cyrillic script.

100

Captain John Summers. Intelligence Corps. 10350556. See file D4/9074/GB/ 94–105.

Kretski looked up at Pomerenko. 'I don't understand.' Pomerenko laughed. 'It's taken a long time, comrade.' He looked at his watch. 'We'd better go.'

They had taken his briefcase and in the black *Chaika* that took them back to Moscow nobody spoke a word.

He sat with his eyes closed, his head resting back on the seat and only stirred as they swept into Dzerzhinski Square.

18

'Tell us about the Malta convoys, Harry.'

The group of men were grinning but Harry Houghton had turned to call for another pint. When it came he turned towards them, glass in hand.

'It was air-cover that was the problem in the Med. We was doing double watches on the guns. Officers and men all had . . .'

'What guns were they, Harry?'

'Oerlikons. Twin turrets fore and aft. We had DEMS gunners. When we got to Valletta they had the Royal Marines band lined up on the harbour to play us in. "White Cliffs of Dover" they played and "Auld Lang Syne".'

'I though you said last time that it was the Black Watch played you in. A piper and "Flowers of the Forest".'

'That was another time, Lofty.'

'Tell us about the Maltese girls, Harry. When you went to the party the day you tied up.'

'They were fantastic those Maltese birds. You had to watch your step, mind you. Try it on the wrong one and you'd have her brothers sticking knives in you. But there was girls. Kids of fourteen and fifteen, real pretty ones. You could have 'em all night for a quid. But if you came in on the relief convoys it was all free. We was heroes to those poor bastards. Starving they was and we brought the food to them through thick and thin. I went to this party and Jesus they were all over me. Took me in the back room. Two of 'em. We was at it all night.'

The men laughed and one of them said, 'Have another pint on me, Harry, you old bullshitter.'

'I'm not bullshitting, I swear. You ask the others.'

'What others?'

'The lads on the Malta convoys. They didn't give Malta the George Cross for nothing, mate.'

The man grinned. 'And no bloody sailor ever got it for free off of a Maltese bird neither.'

Houghton grinned. 'Depends on who you are, mate. Anyway, I gotta be on my way.'

'Your divorce come through yet, Harry?'

'Two months ago, skipper. Foot-loose and fancy free. That's me.'

As he stood outside the pub he turned up his coat collar. It was beginning to snow. He put his head down and walked down the empty promenade. He could hear the waves crashing slowly and heavily on the shingle on the beach. The wind caught his face as he turned into a side road, and five minutes later he passed the permanently open gates to the plot of waste land where his trailer was parked.

He pulled out his keys and turned towards the faint light from the street lamps to sort out the key to the trailer door. He turned to put the key in the door and a hand clamped round his wrist. He turned quickly and saw the man. He looked a real thug and when he spoke he had a Cockney accent.

'Are you Houghton?'

'Yes. Who are you?'

The man put his big leather-gloved fist in front of Houghton's face, and as Houghton instinctively backed away a pair of strong arms went around him from the other side and he realised that there were two of them.

'What the hell's going on?'

'Open the trailer door. Look slippy.'

Houghton's hand shook as he fitted the key into the lock and then one of them opened the door and shoved him up the steps and inside.

'Put the light on.'

Houghton switched the light on and turned to face the two men. The tall one said, 'Why didn't you telephone when you got the Hoover leaflet?'

'I don't understand. Who are you?'

'We brought you a message, sonny boy.'

'What . . .'

And he groaned as the knee went into his crotch. And then the two of them worked him over. Carefully, professionally, leaving his face unmarked as the blows thudded into his stomach and kidneys. Even after they had finished and they stood panting, looking down at his body on the floor, he was still half-conscious and he heard one of them say, 'Next time we'll do your old woman as well. The new one. So watch it, mate.'

It was four o'clock when he came to. The light was still on inside the trailer but the street lights were out. They had left the door open and snow had drifted onto the shabby linoleum. He groaned as he slowly picked himself up.

He made himself a hot whisky and stirred in a spoonful of sugar and lay down in his clothes on the bunk. The light still on, the door of the trailer still open and swinging in the wind.

19

When Shapiro got the news he had called Morton immediately and they were still in Morton's smoke-filled office at four the following morning. Ashtrays full of cigarette ends and cigar butts, trays full of coffee cups, two jugs of cold coffee and several plates with a variety of curling sandwiches.

They had talked for hours, sat silent for minutes at a time and they were no nearer to a solution and no nearer to deciding what to do. They were sprawled in the leather armchairs around a low glass-topped table.

Morton started them off again. 'Let's go over it again, Joe. Piece by piece. Agreed?'

Shapiro nodded and shifted in his seat to try and get comfortable again.

Morton sighed. 'So. Back to square one, Joe. Are they absolutely certain that he's been picked up?'

'He was supposed to ring the Moscow number that evening at nine local time. Just ring and they would give the password. Just that one word and then they'd both hang up. He didn't ring.'

'What about the Warsaw end?'

'We know he got on the airport bus. We know he was at the airport. The girl was watching him and when the call came he went to the correct boarding gate. That was the last time he was seen.'

'What happened at Sheremetyevo?'

'Our guy watched for the plane. Just as a routine check. There was no contact intended.' He paused. 'The flight number was never called and there was no flight from

Warsaw announced or accounted for until the following morning. And that was the normal 9 a.m. flight from Paris and Warsaw.'

'So not only our boy missing but a whole planeload of passengers missing?'

'Yes.'

'Any indications of a crash anywhere on that route?'

'No. But you know what they're like about air disasters.'

'Could it have been diverted because of bad weather?'

'I got Met to check. They say there was heavy snow and some wind but nothing that wasn't normal for the time of year.'

'Where would they divert to if there had been a problem?'

'God knows. There are a dozen or more airfields around Moscow that could take an old Antonov. And they could have diverted to some place way out of Moscow.'

'No way of checking if there was a diversion?'

'RAF intelligence say no. Even internal domestic flights in Warsaw Pact countries are classified. And we haven't got good enough contacts anyway.'

Morton nodded. 'There's one good indication.'

'Tell me.'

'If they'd picked him up and he'd talked they would have tried phoning that number – and they didn't.'

'It was a bit early for that.'

'Agreed, but it weighs against any thoughts he might have defected.'

Shapiro shrugged without speaking and Morton said, 'Was he in Moscow to do anything top-grade?'

'No. Not as far as I know. It was just a routine visit as liaison officer.'

'So why the telephone contact?'

'Routine. A precaution.'

There was another long silence and then Morton said, 'So we're left with deciding whether we do nothing – or something – and if something – what?'

106

'There are only two things we can do. We can't make an official diplomatic complaint. He's officially – genuinely – a Polish national. We've got no diplomatic standing in the case. We could try an unofficial deal and admit that he was ours. Or we could offer an exchange.'

Morton shook his head. 'We haven't got anybody in the bag who's anywhere near an equivalent. Put half a dozen together and they aren't worth offering to Moscow. They'd just laugh at us.'

'Diplomatic pressure?'

Morton laughed harshly. 'Our masters wouldn't go along with it. Détente is the reigning policy. The FO were never informed about the operation in the first place.' He shrugged. 'But they were bloody glad to get the stuff he provided.' He shook his head, sighing. 'Forget 'em, they wouldn't lift a finger to help us.

'Apart from all that we can't really make any move until we know that he's in the bag, and that they've broken him. We could be confirming their suspicions if he hasn't talked already. I recommend that we do nothing except keep a close monitoring of the situation.'

When Morton finished Shapiro looked at him. 'What do you think?'

'How many people know about Phoenix?'

'You, me, Sir Peter and FO liaison, Saunders.'

'Nobody in the FO. Not the Foreign Secretary?'

'No. Nobody. There's been a change of government since we launched Phoenix and the previous Foreign Secretary's dead. We've always tried to treat it as just a piece of routine operations.'

'What about CIA?'

'We share his material with them and they value it highly – but they've no idea of the source. When they've pressed to know we've always implied that it was a Polish national.'

Morton sighed and said, 'So I still recommend we do nothing until we know more. A lot more.'

'I agree.'

107

Morton looked across at Shapiro. 'I understand your concern, Joe, but we could easily make things worse for him.'

Shapiro shook his head slowly. 'It haunts me, Hughie. Right this minute he could be lying in a cell in the Lubyanka after the first beating-up. Hoping against hope that we can do something.'

'You warned him I assume?'

'Of course. All the usual crap. But no matter what we say they never really believe that we'll leave them to rot. Others, yes. Them, no. They're special.' He sighed. 'They never really grasp that once they're in the bag they're not special. Just an embarrassment. Not even a problem. You just forget 'em. At least that's how it's supposed to be.' Shapiro looked at Morton. 'He was so brave, Hughie. All the guts in the world. I'd give everything I've got in the world to get him out. Ten years of his life. Taking risks every day. For us. And it ends like this. No medals, no bloody anything.'

'Take consolation where you can. He may not be in the bag at all. Just some aviation cock-up.'

'I wish I could think that, Hughie. But I can't.' Shapiro stood up, sighing. 'We'd better get on our way. I need some sleep to clear my mind.' But Morton noticed the tears in Shapiro's pale blue eyes. He made a mental note to keep close to Shapiro until things had been sorted out. Deep concern was one thing. Tears were something else. And with a temperament like his there was no knowing what he could get up to.

20

Having been charged with being an illegal alien Emil Goldfus was flown down to the McAllen Alien Detention Facility in Texas. All concerned had recognised that it was only luck that had allowed them to wriggle off the horns of a legal dilemma. If Goldfus had been arrested for espionage he would have been entitled to an almost immediate hearing on that charge and with Reino Hayhanen refusing to testify in court the government had no case. But having arrested him as an illegal alien it meant that the evidence of espionage found in his room was inadmissible. The search was out of bounds for a mere illegal entry charge. Fortunately by the time the judge issued the warrant to search Goldfus's studio Hayhanen had changed his mind.

As the investigators and the prosecution lawyers again went over Hayhanen's statements and questioned every statement as rigorously as he would be questioned by defence counsel in court, the exact location of every 'drop' was established and photographed. Their main difficulty was Hayhanen's desperately poor English.

At first they saw him as just being of low intelligence but they realised as the days passed that in fact he had an excellent memory and was quite astute. What concerned them subconsciously was that despite his vices of drink and women and his total lack of interest in the mission he had been sent on, the United States security services had known nothing about him nor his organiser, Emil Goldfus.

By midsummer the man who now officially admitted to being Rudolph Ivanovich Abel, colonel, KGB, was brought before the grand jury. The main evidence was given by Reino Hayhanen, with other testimony from people who had just happened to be neighbours or acquaintances of Abel.

Finally came the indictment. It charged Rudolph Ivanovich Abel, also known as Mark and Martin Collins and Emil R. Goldfus, of conspiracy on three counts. The first count was conspiring to transmit information relating to the national defence of the USA, particularly arms, equipment and disposition of the armed forces, and the atomic energy programme. The second count was conspiring to gather that information, and the third count was that he had remained in the country without registering as a foreign agent. The third count sounded both strange and faintly ridiculous to the public, but it had its purpose. The penalty for failing to register is five years in prison. To be classed as a foreign agent did not necessarily imply that a person was an intelligence agent. They may merely represent some foreign company or interest and only have as their objective the lobbying of some influential group in government or politics generally. But in the case of Colonel Abel the media made clear that they, at least, had no doubt as to what sort of 'foreign agent' Abel was. The second count could mean ten years' imprisonment and the first count carried the death penalty.

The afternoon newspapers and TV were grateful for such a story in the dog days of summer and the headlines left their readers in no doubt that this was the spy capture of all time. The probability that the colonel would be executed if convicted was also emphasised. The vigilance of the security services was highly commended.

When Abel told the court that he had no lawyer Judge Abruzzo said a lawyer should be appointed and the trial was set for September 16, to be held in the Brooklyn Federal Court before Judge Mortimer W. Byers.

The Bar Association chose wisely. James B. Donovan, an alumnus of Harvard Law School, had been an intelligence officer in the US Navy during World War II, and a member of OSS. He had also been on the staff of the

110

US prosecutor at the Nuremberg Trials. Arnold Fraiman and Tom Dibevoise were appointed as his assistants.

They set out to examine everything that had happened between June 21, the day of Abel's arrest and August 7, when he was indicted by the grand jury. They immediately moved to have everything that had been taken from the hotel declared inadmissible at the trial on the grounds that it had been illegally seized, contrary to the Fourth and Fifth Amendments to the Constitution. An inept statement to the press just after the arrest, by the Commissioner of Immigration, stating that the arrest was made at the specific request of 'several government agencies', added weight to their submission.

The defence was also entitled to all the evidence that the prosecution would be offering and that included an interview with the prosecution's 'mystery man' – Reino Hayhanen. At the interview with the defence lawyers Hayhanen quoted, and insisted on sticking to, his legal rights not to talk until the trial.

The hearing of the motion submitted by the defence was to reveal the main thrust of the case against Abel, but when it came to identification of the items from the hotel room that the defence wanted excluded, Judge Byers had been irritated by both sides' fencing in their approach. When Donovan asked a prosecution witness, 'And did you find any documentary evidence of his status as an alien?', prosecution counsel interrupted, 'I think he should just ask what was found in the hotel room.'

Judge Byers: 'I agree.' He looked at Donovan. 'The witness doesn't need to give his opinion as to the nature of the papers in the evidentiary sense. Ask him what he found.'

'Your honour, this is extremely important.'

Judge Byers shrugged, his irritation all too obvious.

'All right, *don't* ask him what he found. I am telling you what I would like to have you do. Of course, you can disregard my instructions: I realise that.'

Donovan turned again to the witness. 'What did you find in the room that confirmed the information that the FBI had given you?'

Judge Byers intervened. 'The witness does not need to characterise the probative nature of the documents.'

'Agreed, Your Honour, but he did make the statement.'

'I know you like to argue, we all like to argue. Will you just move along.'

Donovan tried to put the question to the witness again and Judge Byers cut him off.

'I am not going to listen to the witness's opinion as to what those documents show. Now take that from me.'

Eventually Donovan argued that the arrest was not made in good faith and that the search and seizure were illegal.

Judge Byers told him bluntly that it was not part of the court's duty to tell the FBI how they should function.

On October 11, Donovan's motion to suppress the evidence was denied. The case could go to trial.

One of the strange features behind the legal wrangling was that Abel was liked, and in some cases admired, by all those who came in contact with him. Prisoners, officials and lawyers found him both mild in manner and extremely intelligent. Their reaction to the man accused of being a Soviet spy was much the same as his friends and neighbours at the Ovington Building.

Tomkins, the prosecutor, was happy about the evidence but was worried about how Reino Hayhanen would react under interrogation and coming face to face with Abel and identifying him as a Soviet spy. But Tomkins made his opening speech to the jury with confidence and authority.

Later he listened to Donovan's speech for the defence and it confirmed his expectation that Donovan would try to discredit Hayhanen's evidence. He closed his eyes and listened intently as Donovan stated the defence case.

'The defendant is a *man*, a man named Abel,' Donovan said. 'It is important that you keep that fact uppermost in your mind throughout the days to come. This is not a case against Communism. It is not a case against Soviet Russia. Our grievances against Russia have been voiced every day in the United Nations and other forums. But the sole issues in this case . . . whether or not Abel has been proved guilty beyond a reasonable doubt of the specific crimes with which he is now charged.'

Half an hour later Tomkins was listening intently as Donovan started his attack on Hayhanen.

'The prosecution has told you that among the principal witnesses against the defendant will be a man whose name is Hayhanen, who claims that he helped the defendant to spy against the United States . . . I want you to observe his demeanour very carefully when he takes the stand.

'Bear in mind that if what the government says is true, it means that this man has been here for some years, living among us, spying on behalf of Soviet Russia . . . It means that he entered the United States on false papers . . . that he has lived here every day only by lying about his true identity, about his background, about every fact of his everyday life . . . He was trained in the art of deception . . . He was trained to lie. In short, assuming that what the government say is true, this man is a professional liar.'

Some observers thought it was odd that neither the prosecution nor the media pointed out that every word of Donovan's derogatory references to Hayhanen applied equally to Rudolph Abel. Tomkins was saving the point for a more effective stage in the proceedings.

When Hayhanen took the stand the courtroom and the media listened to the details of 'drops' and secret signs in places they knew well. It was an amalgam of every spy story they had read and every spy film they had seen. A lamp-post in Riverside Park at 74th Street, another lamp-post near 80th Street. A cinema in Flushing. Drawing-pins in the slat of a park bench. Mail boxes on Central Park West in the upper 70s used for magnetic containers, others on every street corner between 74th and 79th Streets. A fence around the Museum of Natural

History and a 'drop' at a 95th Street subway station. Meetings and journeys with Abel. Abortive attempts to trace and contact American citizens named by Moscow as potential collaborators.

Then followed descriptions of meetings or conversations with Abel about his links with Americans already serving prison sentences for passing information to the Soviet Union. Information concerning atomic and military secrets. Day after day the jury listened to the paraphernalia of espionage. Impressed but confused. Amazed that it could have gone on for so many years apparently without detection.

For four days Donovan, for the defence, cross-examined Hayhanen, trying to discredit his evidence, but Hayhanen was immovable. He insisted vehemently that everything he had said had happened. In one last effort Donovan sought to discredit Hayhanen himself. Questioning him about his lies to Abel about his work, his lies about the money he received, and his lies to get more. But Hayhanen just admitted quite openly to it all. Unabashed and unashamed.

When Donovan referred to the fact that Hayhanen had a wife in Russia but had married another woman, a church marriage, Hayhanen was riled to the point of complaining to the judge about Donovan's questions. It seemed that he didn't care about being accused as a liar, a thief, a coward and a drunkard, but Donovan's smug hypocrisy about his morals clearly enraged him.

On the last day but one of the trial Donovan made his summation. He had one last card to play. He went back over the trial item by item. Then he paused for a moment before looking at the jury.

'What evidence of national defence information or atomic information has been put before you in this case? When you and I commenced this case, certainly we expected evidence that this man is shown to have stolen great military secrets, secrets of atomic energy and so on . . . '

114

Judge Byers interrupted to point out that the charge was only conspiracy to get such information. He turned to Donovan and said, 'The charge doesn't involve a substantial offence. When you undertake to tell the jury what the law is, be accurate in your statements please.'

Donovan turned to a comparison of the characters of Abel and Hayhanen. The dissolute, dishonest drunkard and Abel, the devoted husband, the family man . . . a very brave patriotic man serving his country. He ended his summation with a warning to the jury.

'You are not serving your country and you are not fighting Communism to convict a man on insufficient evidence.' He paused and went on. 'Ladies and gentlemen if you will resolve this case on that higher level so that you can leave it with a clear conscience, I have no question but that certainly on counts one and two in this indictment, you must bring in a verdict of not guilty.'

Then Donovan sat down. His reference to Abel as a family man had had some effect. During the trial letters had been read from his wife and family that had been enlarged from micro-dots found in his studio. They could possibly have been coded messages but they had an authenticity that was convincing. They seemed to be letters from a wife and daughter to an obviously much-loved father. They described the humdrum incidents of domestic life and emphasised how much he was missed. Several observant people had noticed that when the letters were read out there were tears in Abel's eyes. The only indication of any emotion by the prisoner during the whole of the trial.

Tomkins was aware of the sympathy that the letters might arouse and covered it in his final speech. He reminded the jury of the many items of evidence and then went on to remind them of the significance of conspiracy.

'If we agree – if two persons agree, to assassinate the President, and one of them procures a gun, that would be all you needed to complete the crime of conspiracy, and it does not need to be completed to be a crime.' He paused to emphasise his next words. 'In other words, we don't have to stand idly by and permit an individual to commit espionage, to get our secrets. We are not powerless in that case. We can intervene. We can prevent the consummation of the crime.'

Tomkins then referred to Donovan's disparaging description of Hayhanen as 'bum', 'renegade', 'liar', and 'thief' and used it to counter the letters from Abel's family.

'The witness had the same training as the defendant . . .' He went on to point out the difference in their backgrounds, the hapless Hayhanen left to scavenge as best he could, and then reminded them that it appeared from the letters read out in court that Abel's family lived very well in Moscow, with a second home in the country, and servants. He went on to say, 'The defendant is a professional, a highly trained espionage agent . . . a master spy, a real pro . . . Just remember this was the man's chosen career. He knows the rules of the game and so do his family. He is entitled to no sympathy.'

Tomkins looked down at his papers for a moment as he collected his thoughts for his final comment. He looked at the jury for several seconds before he spoke.

'I simply say this: this is a serious case. This is a serious offence. This is an offence directed at our very existence and through us at the free world and civilisation itself, particularly in the light of the times.' He paused. 'And I say this, and I don't believe I have ever said anything with more sincerity or more seriously: I am convinced that the government has proven its case, not only beyond a reasonable doubt as required, but beyond all possible doubt.'

Tomkins sat down with his face still turned to the jury.

On the Friday morning Judge Byers went over again the difference between conspiracy to commit a substantive crime and the crime itself.

At mid-day the jury and the US marshals in charge of them left for the jury room.

It was almost five o'clock when the jury filed back to their seats in the courtroom. The clerk of the court rose, and the foreman of the jury looked back at him.

'Members of the jury, have you agreed upon a verdict?'

'We have.'

'In the case of the United States of America against Rudolph Abel, how do you find the defendant, guilty or not guilty on count one?'

'Guilty.'

'How do you find the defendant, guilty or not guilty on count two?'

'Guilty.'

'How do you find the defendant, guilty or not guilty on count three?'

'Guilty.'

Rudolph Abel was taken to West Street jail to wait for sentencing.

Inevitably Donovan and his team put in a carefully considered submission to the Court of Appeals contending that there were aspects of law that had been ignored at the trial. On July 11, 1958 Judge Watkinson, in a written opinion, rejected the appeal. But not without praising Donovan and his team for 'having represented the appellant with rare ability and in the highest tradition of their profession'.

There was one last weapon in the defence's armoury and Donovan filed a petition for *certiorari* to the Supreme Court. It listed six points of law which Donovan suggested had been ignored or avoided in the trial. He asked that the Supreme Court should grant a hearing for those points to be argued. In October the Supreme Court announced that it would grant a hearing on two points. Both points covered the old original problem of the search and seizure of evidence when Abel was arrested.

In prison in Atlanta, Georgia, Abel was a model prisoner. At that time Joseph Valachi, Vito Genovese and other figures from the Mafia were also serving sentences of various lengths in the same prison. The prison Warden had no problems with Abel, who behaved like the senior officer that he was, and the Warden assumed that Abel had been trained in methods of survival in case he was captured. Both mental and physical survival.

Meanwhile, in New York, both sides filed arguments and counter-arguments. Towards the end of February Donovan presented his case and a month later the Supreme Court handed down its decision. Everybody on the defence and Abel himself were surprised by the decision. It seemed to bode well for the prisoner in Atlanta. The court ordered a re-argument and asked each side to appear on October 12.

More briefs were fired back and forth by both the government and the defence. What the Supreme Court wanted to hear were both sides' arguments on those aspects of Constitutional protection that affected not only the present case but the future interpretation of the current law.

The law gave every citizen 'the right to be secure from searches for evidence to be used in *criminal proceedings*'. Nine eminent judges of the Supreme Court listened to the arguments from both sides.

It was not until March 28, 1960, the following year, that the Supreme Court gave its ruling. The Supreme Court upheld the conviction of Rudolph Ivanovich Abel. But what surprised all concerned was that five judges had upheld the conviction but four had given dissenting opinions. And one of the four dissenters was Chief Justice Warren himself.

After two and a half years in prison in Atlanta Abel himself had changed. People who had known him for a long time said that he had become frail and sick, consumed by tension as if he had been waiting for something that he no longer expected to happen.

21

The plane stood on the tarmac of the parking bay at the airfield in Peshawar, Pakistan, half concealed in its enormous hangar. With its long body, high tail and unusually wide wings its elegance was not obvious because it was painted black. On the drawing board at Lockheed it looked like a smooth, sleek flying fish, but on the ground, in its strange livery, it looked more like a killer shark. It carried no guns, but a mass of infra-red cameras and electronics.

It could photograph a section of the earth's surface 125 miles wide and 3,000 miles long. And photo-interpreters looking at the huge enlargements of the 40,000 paired frames could read the headlines of a newspaper taken from ten miles above the earth. It was believed to be beyond the reach of even the most sophisticated attack planes available to the Soviet Union. It was one of three identical planes used in Operation Overflight, an operation that had already been working successfully and fruitfully for almost four years.

The only unusual feature of the flight that day – May 1, 1960 – was that it was the first flight which would cross the whole of the Soviet Union. Taking off from Peshawar and landing almost 4,000 miles away at Bod in Norway, it would pass over important targets that had never been photographed before.

Rumour had it that the flight was to ensure that when President Eisenhower met President Khrushchev shortly he would be fully up-to-date on Soviet military dispositions.

Inevitably, USAF intelligence officers had considered what routines should apply if a pilot was shot down or force landed in Soviet territory. The plane itself was protected by a timed destruction system. The pilots were offered a cyanide tablet and a silver dollar with a small metal loop so that it could be fastened to a key chain or a chain around the wrist or neck. If the loop was unscrewed it revealed a thin needle whose minute grooves were laced with curare, an instant killer. Taking and using either or both was entirely the pilot's option. They were merely available. Most pilots carried neither but on that particular morning the young, crew-cut pilot when asked if he wanted the silver dollar had taken it, seeing it as a useful weapon rather than a means of committing suicide.

That morning the pilot stood at the table in the hangar with the intelligence officer as he was handed the various standard items for a flight. Shaving kit, civilian clothes, a packet of filter cigarettes, pictures of his wife, some German marks, Turkish lira, Russian roubles, gold coins, watches and rings for barter, a hundred US dollars, US postage stamps, a Defense Department ID card, a NASA certificate, instrument rating cards, US and International driving licences, a Selective Service card, a social security card, and an American flag poster that said in fourteen different languages 'I am an American'.

For the last time they traced his route on the maps. From Peshawar he would cross Afghanistan and the Hindu Kush and enter Soviet airspace near Stalinabad. Then over the Aral Sea, the Turyatam missile testing base, Chelyabinsk, Sverdlovsk, Kirov, Archangel, Kandalaksha and Murmansk on the Kola peninsula, then across the Barents Sea to the north coast of Norway and Bod. The flight would take nine hours, and for three-quarters of the time would be inside the USSR. During the nine-hour flight there would be complete radio silence.

The only qualms the twenty-seven-year-old pilot had were about the plane itself. The plane which had previously been reserved for the flight had been grounded at the last moment for a maintenance check, and its substitute, Number 360, was what the pilots referred to as a 'dog'. There was always something going wrong with it, most recently its fuel tanks had malfunctioned and wouldn't feed fuel to the engine. It was a single-engined turbojet.

May 1, 1960 was a Sunday and the pilot got into the plane at 5.30 a.m. for the pre-flight check. The scheduled take-off time was 6 a.m. but it came and went without the signal to go.

The cockpit was like a furnace and the pilot sat with his long underwear drenched in perspiration as he waited. A senior officer came over to apologise for the delay and to explain that they were awaiting final approval for the flight from the White House. Presidential approval normally came through well before the pilot was locked in his seat.

It was twenty minutes later when the plane took off and when it was at flight altitude the pilot completed his flight log entries: aircraft number 360, sortie number 4154 and the time was 6.26 a.m. local time, 1.26 Greenwich Mean Time, 8.26 p.m. in Washington and 3.26 a.m. in Moscow.

As he crossed into Soviet territory he saw several con trails of aircraft way below him but he knew they wouldn't even be able to get near him. He guessed that Soviet radar might have picked him up on their screens and were sending up scouts. A waste of time at his altitude.

Some thirty miles east he could see the launching pads of the Turyatam Cosmodrome where they launched the Soviet Sputniks and ICBMs. He flipped the camera switches to 'on' and only switched them off when the cloud cover thickened again. Fifty miles south of Chelyabinsk the skies cleared and he got a wonderful view of the snow-capped Urals.

It was then that the trouble started; the auto-pilot seemed to have gone berserk and the plane was pitching and yawing nose-up. He switched off the auto-pilot and drove the plane manually for twenty minutes before he switched to auto-pilot again. And again the plane was pitching nose-up. He tried it again at intervals and always with the same result. He decided to stay on manual and make long zigs and zags. He was making notes in his log of the engine and instrument behaviour when he felt a dull thud. The plane bucked forward and a blinding flash of orange light flooded the cockpit.

He reached for the destruction switches and then decided to get into position to use the ejection seat first, but the metal canopy rail was trapping his legs. Ejecting in those conditions would slice off both his legs about three inches above the knee. The plane was already down to 30,000 feet when he released his seat-belt. The force of gravity snatched him half out of his seat, only his oxygen hoses were holding him back. He had forgotten to release them. He kicked and wrestled in panic until he was sucked out of the cockpit and found himself floating free. At the moment when he realised that he had not pulled the ripcord his body jerked as, at 15,000 feet, his parachute opened automatically. At that moment he saw his plane hurtling past him, intact, towards the earth.

The following Thursday Nikita Khrushchev showed all the peasant cunning that had been rather admired in the West. He addressed the Supreme Soviet for over three hours during which he announced that Soviet gunners had shot down a US plane violating Soviet airspace. He went on to denounce the United States in aggressive abuse, accusing them of deliberately trying to wreck the forthcoming summit conference between the four heads of government.

The following day, to the delight of the Kremlin, Lincoln White, the State Department's spokesman, announced to crowds of journalists in Washington, that 'There was absolutely no – N – O – no deliberate intention to violate Soviet airspace, and there never had been.' President Eisenhower confirmed the statement later the same day.

The next day Khrushchev told the Supreme Soviet what some of them already knew – a Soviet rocket had brought down the plane from an altitude of 65,000 feet. And then the final blow for the White House, the US pilot had been taken prisoner 'alive and kicking' and had made a complete confession about his spying mission.

A few days later Khrushchev said, at a display of the U-2 wreckage, 'The Russian people would say I was mad to negotiate with a man who sends spy planes over here.'

The turmoil and embarrassment in the White House and the State Department were there for all to see. Not only had they put the summit conference at risk but had been caught out in a flagrant lie. And the President of the United States had himself lied in public.

Nevertheless, on May 14 Khrushchev arrived in Paris. His first move was to announce that he would not participate in the summit unless the United States stopped all U-2 flights, apologised for past aggressions and punished those responsible for the flight.

President Eisenhower said in public that the flights had been suspended and would not be resumed. But even the humbling of the President was not enough for Khrushchev. At the opening session of the conference at the Elysée Palace with President Eisenhower, President de Gaulle and Prime Minister Harold Macmillan, Khrushchev suggested that the conference should be postponed for six months and accused the President of the United States of 'treachery' and 'acts of banditry', and announced the cancellation of the arranged visit of Eisenhower to the USSR.

A grim-faced Eisenhower replied that the over-flights were over but that Khrushchev's ultimatum was unacceptable to the United States. And at that point Khrushchev stormed out of the conference. Eisenhower went back into the US Embassy trembling with rage.

Eisenhower, de Gaulle and Macmillan held an informal, broken-backed meeting the next day, and the summit was over.

But Khrushchev's revenge was far from over. Three thousand journalists and broadcasters attended a chaotic press conference the next day when Khrushchev denounced the United States as 'piratical', 'thief-like', and 'cowardly'. He followed this diatribe by announcing that the Soviet Union would now solve the Berlin problem by signing a separate treaty with communist East Germany.

22

The long line of cattle-trucks stretched right across the horizon, silhouetted by the setting sun and black against the first scattering of the coming winter's snow.

In one of the tail-end wagons a man sat hunched up in a corner, his legs drawn up, his head resting on his knees, his dark hair lank and long, his cheeks flushed with fever. There were forty other prisoners in the wagon. Five of them frozen stiff, to be thrown out by the guards the next time they checked the prisoners.

The train had been on its journey for two weeks already and of the 1,650 who had started the journey 60 had already died.

Five days later the prisoners were herded onto the steamer *Dzhurma* for the voyage across the Sea of Okhotsk. If they were lucky they would complete the voyage before the pack-ice closed in around Wrangel Island. If the transport authorities guessed wrong and the ice closed in, that would mean that there would be no prisoner survivors from that shipment. The Gulag authorities in Moscow and Kolyma considered it a worthwhile risk. Once the pack-ice formed, the steamer would be locked-in until the spring thaw. But Gulag labour camps needed their new replacements if they were to meet their norms. Leaving it late could generally mean pushing through four extra shipments, and even with the chance of a twenty-five per cent loss that was a reasonable return.

The man in the corner was going through the litany that had kept him alive and as near to sanity as he could hope for. Amid the stench of excreta and urine

125

he went again and again through the Lord's Prayer, half a dozen hymns, Gray's 'Elegy in a Country Churchyard' and Wordsworth's 'Daffodils', the names of the home grounds of every first-class football club that he could remember, the instructions for clearing a blockage on a Bren gun, odd bits of the Bible and Shakespeare, Boyle's Law on expansion of gases and the names of the girls he had slept with. Sometimes he thought of the password, but he never said it, or even let it linger in his mind. It was best forgotten, but you can't forget just because you want to.

He could smell the pus from the weals on his back and ribs. They'd offered him a course of antibiotics in return for what he knew about Mark Wheeler and Tony Craddock. The instructors had always said that beating-up and torture never produced useful information and that the beatings and pain only stiffened a prisoner's resistance. He had smiled when he had heard it and hadn't believed a word of it. A broken finger or two, a rough hand round your scrotum or even the bath treatment, and you'd be singing like a nightingale. Maybe it applied to ex-Shanghai police instructors but not to ordinary mortals. But the bastards were right. Once you'd got over the shock of being caught it wasn't the pain that counted but the fact that they were doing it to you that sat in the front of your mind. It was a fight even though you couldn't move. You could hit back by saying nothing. Screaming maybe but not talking. Name, rank and number stuff taken to ridiculous extremes. Just hate the bastards and shout obscenities in their own language. And it wouldn't take long before they went too far and you were out. Sailing on white cumulus clouds in a summer sky, the wolves below snapping at your gliding body until you floated past the cliff and out over the sea.

There was a week in the transit camp at Vladivostok before the sea voyage to the horror camp at Kolyma, where tens of thousands laboured in the gold mines. Men, women and children were the victims of disease

126

and a regime of systematic cruelty that rivalled the worst excesses of the Nazi concentration camps. Three million of the stream of hopeless prisoners had died in Kolyma, their graves unmarked because there were no graves. A tractor gouged out a few feet of frozen earth and then shovelled the daily quota of corpses into the pit, skeletal hands, feet and sometimes heads were left projecting when the permafrost set the earth iron-hard, chopped off later by a mechanical grader.

John Summers had been put in a separate enclosure with three other special grade prisoners. Two of them had no legs and the third was blind. At night the barbed-wire compound was permanently floodlit. Day after day Summers was detailed to collect all the new corpses and deliver them on a flat barrow to the guardroom for registration. The routine was simple. The name and prison number were recorded with the date of death, the duty guard thrust his bayonet into the silent heart of the already dead prisoner and the corpse was stripped and thrown onto the pile of other bodies to await the next mass-burial.

23

Harris was in a hurry but he went into the information
room and signed that he had checked the weekly information files laid out on the table. As he headed for the door
he stopped, hesitating, and then, sighing, he walked back
to the table and sat down. No responsible officer signed
that he had read his obligatory files when he hadn't done
so. Out of the dozen or so files there were only three
obligatory files for him. One marked 'USSR', one marked
'CIA/FBI' and a third, a thin file marked 'Australasia'.

There were two file number references in the Soviet
file that he noted and then he reached for the CIA/FBI
file. He had virtually no current contacts with the United
States security services but he read through the two-line
references to other files as he slowly turned the pages.
It was on the third page of photographs that he stopped.
Despite the grainy blow-ups he recognised both faces
immediately. It just said: 'Morris Cohen and Laura
Teresa Cohen. Associate of the Rosenbergs, David
Greenglass, Harry Gold and others. Disappeared from
their address in New York immediately prior to arrest
of Julius Rosenberg. Present whereabouts unknown.
Possible locations, Australia, New Zealand, West or
East Germany, United Kingdom. See Washington file
70410/04/3466. Restricted.'

He was looking at photographs of Peter John Kroger
and Helen Joyce Kroger, antiquarian bookseller and his
quiet suburban wife. The owners of the Rover car that
had been parked at the 'looker's' cottage. Associates of
the mysterious Mr Gordon and the middle-aged woman

from Weymouth and Portland who owned the cream-coloured Mini.

For ten minutes Harris sat there, collecting his thoughts. He knew by instinct that they were no longer just thrashing around. They were in business at last and it meant a radical change in the operation. This latest piece in the jig-saw would warrant a full surveillance organisation. It could mean thirty or more trained people. And that could mean the operation being taken over by Shapiro himself or someone else equally senior. He reached for the internal telephone and dialled Shapiro's number. Shapiro had already left the office but he had left a number where he could be contacted. He dialled the number and Shapiro answered.

'Shapiro. Who is it?'

'It's Harris, sir. I've just come across something that alters my operation.'

'Oh, what is it?'

'A connection, sir. A CIA/FBI connection.'

'Why can't you deal with it?'

'I think it's more your level.'

'Can it wait until the morning? I'll be in early. About eight.'

'I'd rather deal with it tonight if I can.'

He heard the impatience in Shapiro's voice as he said, 'Are you at the office?'

'Yes.'

'I'll be there in fifteen minutes.'

'I can come to you if that's more convenient.'

'I'll be there in fifteen minutes.'

Shapiro was in evening dress: dinner jacket, black tie and four miniature medals. He took Harris's arm and walked to the far side of the reception area. When he came to a halt he said, 'Right, what is it?' He sounded as if he resented being disturbed. He frowned as if whatever he was going to be told was unwelcome.

Harris told him of the CIA/FBI photographs.

129

Shapiro said sharply, 'Are you quite sure? Those photographs are never good quality.'

'Yes, I'm quite sure.'

'We'd better go up to my office.'

As they went up in the lift Harris said, 'I'm sorry I've had to disturb your evening.'

Shapiro didn't respond but in his office he took off his dinner jacket. 'Show me your photographs and the file photographs.'

It was ten minutes before Harris came back with the material and Shapiro looked at both sets of photographs for several minutes before he looked up at Harris.

'Yes. You're right.' He paused and leaned back in his chair, closing his eyes. 'We'll need a twenty-four-hour team for the Cohens' place in Ruislip and the bookshop. Another team for the Gordon chap and the spinster at Weymouth. We'll have to think about Grushko too. Has Grushko got diplomatic status?'

'No. It wasn't requested for him either.'

'We'll pull him in when we pick up the others.'

'What about the MP – Maguire-Barton?'

'Go on checking on him and keep me informed – but leave him for me to deal with.'

'Do you want me to stay in charge of the operation?'

Shapiro looked surprised. 'Do you know of any reason why you shouldn't?'

'I thought that as it was getting bigger you might . . .'

'How many bodies do you want?'

'On my calculations I could get by with thirty. I might need more if it takes long.'

'We might have to call in some outside help if it's a long term job. Special Branch and Five.' He stopped and looked at Harris's face. 'You'd better leave this to me. Go home and get some sleep. You look as if you need it.'

Shapiro was on the phone even before Harris got to

130

the door and he called out, 'Be here at eight, Mr Harris. There'll be people to brief.'

'Yes, sir.'

Harris applied for, and got, an incident room and two clerks to record and collate the information coming in from the surveillance team and other sources. Like most surveillance operations whole days could go by with nothing suspicious reported, but when there were contacts every detail had to be noted. Locations, time, photography where possible, identification, description of the meeting, weather conditions, light conditions and all the rest of the information to rebut defending counsels' insistence in court that the meeting never took place or that the light conditions were too bad for accurate observation.

Harris reported daily to Shapiro who seemed anxious to hurry things along. But there was always one major problem with this kind of surveillance and investigation: they were founded on little more than suspicion, and courts were not interested in suspicion, neither was the Director of Public Prosecutions.

What they wanted was evidence, and, so far as English law was concerned, it had to be evidence not merely of intent to spy but proof of actual espionage. If Soviet diplomats were concerned then suspicion could be enough. They could be declared 'personae non gratae' and sent packing. But 'illegals', who had to come before the courts, were given all the benefits that any other defendant could expect.

24

Once Shapiro had arranged for full surveillance teams Harris deployed them quickly and right at the start they had a lucky break. Farrance, one of the new men, had followed Mr Gordon to a block of luxury flats, the White House, in Regent's Park. And from there to his workplace in Peckham.

Both places had been subjected to covert searches but the searchers found nothing suspicious apart from large sums of money in cash in a false ceiling in the toilet at the flat. The money was sterling and dollars to the value of just over three thousand pounds. But the search revealed that Mr Gordon was, in fact, a Mr Gordon Arnold Lonsdale. Discreet enquiries among some of the customers of the business only confirmed that the business was both successful and efficient. The company had a substantial share of the London gambling machine market, and Mr Lonsdale's partners seemed to be no more than normal businessmen.

A request was sent to the Royal Canadian Mounted Police in Canada for any information on a Gordon Arnold Lonsdale. Suspected of espionage. Two weeks later a report came back that at least established that Lonsdale was travelling on a fake passport. With espionage suspected, the RCMP implemented a routine check on driving licence applications. A Gordon Arnold Lonsdale had applied for one in 1954 giving his address at No. 1527 Burnaby Street, Vancouver. From there he was traced to the address of a boarding house in Toronto. And it was at that point they discovered that he had a Canadian passport.

Corporal Jack Carroll of the RCMP had landed from a British Viscount plane at a snow-covered landing-strip in northern Ontario to check the details of Gordon Arnold Lonsdale in his birthplace – Cobalt, Ontario. It took only three days to reveal that the real Gordon Lonsdale had been taken back to Finland by his mother when he was only three years old. The rest was surmise, but for experienced intelligence officers it wasn't difficult to imagine what had happened. The boy's genuine documents would have been taken by the KGB and used to provide cover for the man calling himself Lonsdale. It was a normal KGB practice. But above all they now had legitimate grounds for picking up Lonsdale and charging him, any time they wanted. But they wanted to challenge him with a lot more than using a false passport.

The check on Ethel Gee showed that she had started work at the Underwater Weapons Establishment at Portland in 1950, and she had signed the Official Secrets Act document that all civil servants have to sign if they are engaged on any secret work. She was forty-six and she lived in Hambro Road, Portland, Devon.

Her boy-friend was fifty-five. He was Henry Frederick Houghton and he lived not far from Gee in Meadow View Road, Broadway, a suburb of Weymouth. He was employed at the same establishment as Gee and was responsible for the distribution and filing of all papers and documents, including Admiralty Fleet Orders and Admiralty charts. His salary was £741 a year.

The first meeting of all three of them that the surveillance team had covered was on July 9, 1960.

Lukas had followed Houghton to the Cumberland Hotel. Ethel Gee had walked into the foyer through the Oxford Street entrance a few minutes later. She and Houghton had talked for a few moments and then left the hotel taking the Underground to Waterloo Station. Lukas asked for assistance on his pocket radio and Ivan Beech

133

and Lukas followed the couple out of the station. As they approached the Old Vic they were joined by Lonsdale. They obviously all knew one another well. Lonsdale gave Houghton an envelope. A few moments later Houghton left Lonsdale and Gee talking together. When he returned he was carrying a blue paper bag. He took a parcel out of the bag and gave it to Lonsdale.

About five minutes later they split up. Lukas followed Lonsdale, and Beech followed the couple.

Lonsdale had walked to where he had parked his car, frequently looking over his shoulder to see if he was being followed. Twice he had walked past his car before doubling back and driving to his flat.

Houghton and Gee had gone to the Albert Hall for a performance by the Bolshoi Ballet.

The surveillance was stepped up when the evaluation showed that the first Saturday in the month seemed to be a permanent rendezvous for the three of them.

Farrance had been trailing Lonsdale on August 26 when he followed him to Great Portland Street where Lonsdale parked his car and went into the Midland Bank. A few minutes later he came back to his car and took out a brown attaché case and several small packages which he took back into the bank and left with the clerk for safe custody.

Harris had applied for, and got, a search warrant for the attaché case, and the contents had been listed and photographed before the case was returned to the bank.

In the case was a Ronson table-lighter, a Praktica camera, two film cassettes and a bunch of seven keys.

It wasn't until October 24 that Lonsdale reclaimed the case from the bank. He walked to an address in Wardour Street and when he left he was carrying a different brown leather briefcase. Lukas had followed him when he went by Underground from Piccadilly and got off at Ruislip Manor station. From the station he walked to 45,

Cranley Drive and at last there was further confirmation implicating the bookseller.

On Saturday November 5 Houghton was under surveillance in Puddletown in Dorset. When Houghton entered a hotel Farrance saw a large cardboard box and a leather briefcase on the back seat of Houghton's Renault car. Beech and Farrance followed him as he drove to London where he parked his car near a pub called the Maypole. Ten minutes later Lonsdale joined him there carrying a briefcase. A few minutes later Houghton and Lonsdale were driving slowly in Houghton's car. They stopped in the shadows of a group of trees and then drove back to the Maypole. When they left, Lonsdale was carrying a black document case which was not the case he had arrived with. They drove off in Houghton's car and were lost in the traffic at Marble Arch.

Saturday, December 10 linked both sides of Lonsdale's network. In the early afternoon Lonsdale had met Houghton and Gee at their old rendezvous in Waterloo Road and in the early evening Lonsdale had parked his car about twenty-five yards from the Krogers' home in Cranley Drive. It had stayed there until just before noon the following day.

It was decided at a meeting between Morton and MI5 liaison that the arrest of the five suspects and the subsequent handling of the case should revert to MI5 and Special Branch who had been kept informed of the last six months' surveillance.

Shapiro's meeting with Harris had not been smooth.

'You'll be required to give evidence and so will your team but the rest is out of our hands now.'

'But why? They're there for the taking.'

'And Special Branch will take them.'

'But we've done the hard grafting all the way.'

'Which was what you were told to do.'

'How do I explain all this to my chaps who've sweated their guts out for months?'

135

'You don't explain. You send them back to the pool with your congratulations and praise them for a job well done.'

'Can I ask you a very frank question, sir?'

'Yes – but I might not answer it.'

'Was there ever a reason why we – SIS – were told to take on this operation?'

'Yes – a very good reason.'

'You know the reason?'

'Yes. I was one of the three people who made the decision.'

'But *I* can't be told what the reason was?'

'I'm afraid not.'

For a moment Harris locked eyes with his senior and then he turned and headed for the door. As he opened the door Shapiro called out.

'Harris.'

'Sir.'

Shapiro nodded. 'Well done. Keep at it.'

Harris was plainly neither amused nor mollified by the official pat on the back.

The spy network's regular, first Saturday in the month, meeting on January 7 was the last. Houghton had deviated from his usual routine and had parked his car at Salisbury Station and he and Ethel Gee had caught the 12.32 train to Waterloo. The train arrived at 3.20 p.m. At 4.30 Lonsdale arrived outside the Old Vic Theatre, parked his car and stood on the corner of the street. Houghton and Gee crossed from Lower Marsh to where Lonsdale was standing. They walked past him without acknowledging him and he turned and followed them, catching up with them a few moments later.

Gee was carrying a shopping basket and Lonsdale took a parcel from it. It was then that a Special Branch officer walked past them, turning to face them as he said, 'You are under arrest.' The parcel was found to contain four Admiralty Test reports and a cassette of undeveloped

136

film. When it had been processed it was of 230 pages of an Admiralty book entitled 'Particulars of War Vessels'.

At 6.30 p.m. that evening SB officers knocked on the door of 45 Cranley Drive and the Krogers were arrested.

25

When the brief radio message came through that Lonsdale and the others had been arrested and that there was hard evidence of espionage, Shapiro checked with the teams still covering Grushko and Maguire-Barton. Grushko was at his flat and was alone.

When Shapiro rang the bell it was a couple of minutes before Grushko opened the door. Shapiro held up his ID card and Grushko shrugged and looked back at him.

'What is it you want?'

'I'd like to come in and talk to you.' And there was real surprise on Grushko's face when Shapiro responded in Russian. For a moment he hesitated and then he opened the door wider and Shapiro walked in. He had seen photographs of the room way back and it looked much the same.

Grushko said, 'I'll have to leave in ten minutes. What is it you want?'

Shapiro smiled and sat down on the couch as he pointed at an armchair. 'Let's make ourselves comfortable, comrade.'

Grushko sat reluctantly. 'I haven't got much time.'

'It's going to take quite a time, Comrade Grushko, so you might as well relax.'

'What is this all about?'

'Well now. We've got a problem. You've been rather a naughty boy and we're not sure yet what we're going to do about you. You haven't any diplomatic immunity so we could put you on trial, or we could ship you back to Moscow. Or we could just talk – and co-operate – and

138

leave it at that.' Shapiro smiled. 'We don't have a lot of evidence to put before a court. But enough. Enough to show that you've been involved in espionage. You've not been all that successful I'll admit, but it's enough to get you two or three years in prison.' He paused. 'And when we eventually send you back to Moscow they wouldn't be very happy with your performance here. If we just send you back without taking you to court they'll be even more unhappy with your operation in London. We'd just have to let them know that you'd been so amateurish, so inept, that we just smiled at your efforts and sent you back.' He looked at Grushko. 'You do understand what I mean, don't you?'

'What the hell is it you want from me? I don't understand all this . . .' he waved his arm dismissively '. . . all this rubbish.'

'Oh, but you do, Grigor. You know that I'm being very generous with you. Giving you a chance to just go about your journalistic work on Monday morning as if nothing had happened. No trouble from Moscow and no trouble from us.' He paused. 'That is, if you behave yourself in future.'

'What is it you want to know?'

'Let's start with Maguire-Barton. Tell me about him and his relationship with you.'

Grushko shrugged. 'He just wanted a few free trips abroad.'

'So why did he use a faked passport?'

'He thought he might be criticised for taking too many journeys to Warsaw Pact countries.'

'He could have avoided such criticism by not going. So why was it so important to him?'

For long moments Grushko was silent and then he said, 'If I tell you everything do you promise that I'll not be drawn into it and nothing will go back to Moscow?'

'If you co-operate – really co-operate. We're prepared to let you carry on as a journalist for six months. After six months you will tell Moscow that you think that you're under surveillance and you think you should be withdrawn back to Moscow. Tell them that you've had enough of the West and you want to be back in Moscow.'

Grushko seemed to be considering what Shapiro had said and then he took a deep breath. 'Maguire-Barton gave me profiles of Members of Parliament. Their life-styles, their finances, their sexual habits – the usual stuff. And he gave me reports on his colleagues' attitudes to the Soviet Union. Who might be influenced or bribed with money or sex. Nothing more than that. I passed the information to the embassy KGB so that certain MPs could be recruited as agents of influence.'

'Tell me about Lonsdale.'

The Russian looked back at Shapiro, shaking his head. 'I daren't. If I talked about him they'd know that your people could only have got it from me.'

Shapiro said quietly, 'We arrested Lonsdale today. About an hour ago. We've arrested his network too.'

Shapiro could see that the news of Lonsdale's arrest had really shaken the Russian. It was best to let the news sink in.

'When were you recruited to the KGB?'

'I never was.'

'Was it the GRU then?'

'I was never a member of either organisation. I genu-inely am a journalist.' He shrugged. 'But as you know we get used by the KGB for odd jobs from time to time.'

'What did you think of Maguire-Barton?'

'As a man you mean?'

'Yes.'

'He's what we call in Moscow 'a skater'. A chap who just skates on the surface. Likes to be seen around but no real interest in anything. He's a kind of playboy. A political playboy. Likes publicity. Likes women of course. Especially if they help in getting his picture in the papers. He'd like to be a TV personality doing chat-shows. Recognised wherever he goes but not needing any real talent. I think he knows he's second-rate. He's not really

140

ambitious. Just wants the good life. Or what he thinks is the good life.'

'What kind of money did he take?'

'A few thousands a year. Not a lot.' He shrugged and smiled. 'He didn't do a lot either.'

'Did you get receipts for the money?'

'Yes. Moscow wanted to have a hold on him.'

'Have you got them?'

'I've got photocopies.'

Shapiro looked at Grushko's face. 'Anything else you think I should know?'

'You're not bluffing about Lonsdale being arrested?'

'No way.'

'What were the names of the others who were taken?'

'Do you know their names?'

'Yes.'

'OK. They were Harry Houghton, Ethel Gee and a married couple named Kroger.'

Grushko sighed. 'Lonsdale is KGB. I'm not sure what his rank is but it's senior, major or lieutenant-colonel.'

'What was your rôle in the network?'

'I was just a post-box for his material. He's an illegal so he has no contact with our embassy. Not even a KGB contact. He was mainly responsible for getting naval information.'

'What kind of naval information?'

'I've no idea. I should imagine anything he could get.'

'Who ordered you to co-operate with him?'

'Our embassy in Ottawa briefed me. Told me to assist him in any way he needed so long as it didn't compromise my position here.'

'And what did you do for him?'

'I took his material and passed it to the embassy and they forwarded it in the diplomatic bag. They thought it was mine. I arranged meeting places and drops.' He shrugged, 'That's about it.'

'Tell me about him. What sort of fellow is he?'

141

'He's an arrogant bastard. Sees himself as the master-spy. The spider at the centre of the web and all that rubbish.' When Shapiro smiled Grushko said, 'I mean it. I got the impression that Moscow didn't like him much either, so he must have been useful. Women go for him. God knows why. He's an ugly bastard. You've only got to look at his eyes and you'd know that he's a crook. He was a born capitalist. Fancied himself as a tycoon with his tatty little business. He told Moscow it was just as a cover for his movements but it wasn't. He told me he was aiming to be a millionaire. He'd have probably ended up staying here permanently if you hadn't spotted him.'

'Who's your girlfriend? The dark-haired one. Lives in Cardiff.'

'I don't know who you mean. I've never been to Cardiff nor had a girlfriend who lives there.'

'You've been seen with her and she's been to embassy receptions with both you and Maguire-Barton.'

Grushko smiled. 'I know who you mean now. Do trains to Cardiff stop at Birmingham?'

'Most of them do.'

'She's the girlfriend of a Party member who lives in Birmingham. She brings material from him for me and takes instructions back to him.'

'What's his name?'

'Holloway. Jake Holloway.'

'And what does he do?'

'He's a left-wing activist, a lecturer in Birmingham at the university.'

'Tell me about him.'

'I don't remember much about him. He's a friend of Maguire-Barton. He put me in touch with Holloway. Said he was a Marxist activist. I had brief contacts with a lot of these grass-roots types.'

'What sort of contacts?'

Grushko shrugged. 'Sometimes they needed aid but usually they wanted to talk politics.' He half-smiled.

142

'Wanting to tell Moscow how to run our foreign policy.'
He paused. 'Was this fellow bald with a beard?'

'Yes.'

'I remember him now. He saw himself as the leader of the revolution in Britain. Used to give me messages to Gromyko and the Politburo. When was the revolution going to start? Had they forgotten Marx's article in 1855 about tearing off the mask of the bourgeoisie in England? The usual crap these people go in for.'

'Did you pass money to Holloway?'

'I don't remember. I never met one of them who didn't want funds for some wildcat scheme. I gave them small amounts and just kept them happy.'

'Is that all Moscow wanted?'

'Moscow was happy to keep them on the boil. They had a nuisance value.'

'Does Moscow give you leads to these people?'

'With people like Maguire-Barton – yes. But people like Holloway they get in touch with the embassy and if they're not interested they pass them on to me.'

'What do they expect from you?'

Grushko sighed. 'Free trips to Moscow, cash, moral support – whatever feeds their little power struggles.'

'Would Lonsdale be interested in coming over to us?'

'I don't know. I don't know him all that well. I shouldn't think so. He's got a family. And he'd rather play the hero. If you put him in court he'll love it. Every minute of it.'

'Did he have much contact with Maguire-Barton?'

'I'm not sure. They're rather like one another in a lot of ways so they disliked each other.'

Shapiro said quietly, 'Find a reason for going back to Moscow in about six months, Grigor. You'll be quite safe. There'll be no leaks from us. But no more silly games. Stick to the journalism.'

'You give me your word there will be no leaks?'

'Absolutely. Only two other people in SIS even

know that I've been here. There will be no written record.'

'And you've not bugged this place?'

Shapiro smiled. 'Grigor. What a thing to say.'

Sir Peter interviewed Maguire-Barton personally. There was just about enough on the MP for the DPP to mount a court case against him but it was not much more than a long list of contacts with suspect people. Courts didn't like circumstantial evidence in treason charges unless there was at least an attempt to provide actual hard evidence of information being passed that could be considered to endanger the security of the State. A nod from certain quarters of the Establishment was as good as a wink even in the High Court, but there had to be some underlying evidence especially when the MP concerned was a member of the Labour Party, whose left-wing militants would claim that one of the brotherhood was being deliberately harassed in carrying out his normal parliamentary duties.

It was an occasion for the black jacket, pin-striped trousers and a black tie. And the panelled office.

Maguire-Barton was tall, with a quite handsome face, sallow complexion, soft brown eyes and considerable charm. The kind of charm that most men instinctively dislike. Professional and indiscriminate charm. He was mentioned frequently in the gossip diaries, generally as the escort of some minor film actress or débutante. Like any other minor public figure who was unmarried, there were rumours of homosexuality and hints of unprintable predilections, but nobody had ever provided even the faintest substance for such rumours. He was adored by the female contingent who dominated his constituency party and disliked and envied by most of his colleagues in the House of Commons. Disliked by Tories as a social-climbing, self-publicising nonentity, and envied by his fellow Labour MPs for much the same reasons. For a short period he had been the opposition's spokesman on trade and industry but his ill-concealed

144

indifference to the subject had made it a short-lived appointment.

Sir Peter had long years of experience in putting quite senior civil servants and administrators in their place. And he knew from experience that it was the lightweights who were always the most difficult to deal with. The heavyweights mounted a well-argued defence that he was well capable of destroying piece by piece, but lightweights blustered or were indifferent because they didn't know any other way.

When Maguire-Barton was shown in Sir Peter walked from his desk to greet him and show him to the armchair by the marble fireplace. He settled himself comfortably into its twin and looked across at the MP, taking an instant dislike to the brown suit and the flamboyant MCC tie.

'Mr Maguire-Barton. I thought we should have a chat.'

Maguire-Barton smiled. 'Honoured, I'm sure. Please make it Jack. I hate formality.'

'Don't we all. But although this is an informal chat it nevertheless has some formal aspects.'

'Sounds ominous, Sir Peter.'

'Let's talk first about Mr Grushko.'

'Mr Grushko?'

'Yes. Grigor Grushko. A Russian. Calls himself a freelance journalist.'

'Ah yes. A very talented man. And with considerable influence in Moscow I understand.'

'You see a lot of him, don't you?'

'I see him from time to time, as I do a number of members of the press.'

'What other members of the press have you met a couple of dozen times in the last six months?'

The spaniel eyes looked at Sir Peter for several moments before Maguire-Barton replied. 'Are you telling me that I've been watched?' he said softly.

'Observed, let us say.'

'You mean that your people have been checking on the comings and goings of a Member of Parliament?'

'Yes. We keep a protective eye on any MP who has regular contacts with Russians or any other Warsaw Pact people.'

'Have you received any authorisation to do this in my case?'

'I don't need any authorisation to do this, it's part of our standard practice.'

'You mean you waste your people's time on watching an MP who in the normal course of his duties happens to meet foreigners?'

'Depends on the foreigners, Mr Maguire-Barton. And on what they're up to.'

'I shall have to report this to the Prime Minister and I shall certainly ask questions in the House.'

'The Foreign Secretary and the PM already know that I'm interviewing you. And why. And you would be very unwise to raise any questions in Parliament.'

'It happens to be one of my privileges as an MP, Sir Peter.'

'Are you suggesting that regular meetings, both public and private, with a Russian who is a close working associate and collaborator of a senior officer of the KGB in this country, are the privilege of a man just because he's an MP? And that such meetings should be treated differently than they would be if they were by a member of the public?'

'Who says that he's anything to do with the KGB?'

'I say so, Mr Maguire-Barton.'

'You'd have to prove that.'

'I wouldn't. My opinion would be enough.'

'Not for me it wouldn't.'

Sir Peter smiled acidly and said quietly, 'Grushko has already been interviewed. We should be happy to publish the statement he's made concerning his relationship with you.'

'The word of a Russian agent against the word of an MP?'

'You could hardly cast doubt on the veracity of a man with whom you admit that you had such a close and continuous relationship.' He paused. 'And why do you assume that you would want to cast doubt on what he has told us?'

'When was he arrested?'

'I'm afraid I can't discuss such matters with you.' He paused. 'Then there is your relationship with a Mr Holloway, a lecturer at Aston University.'

'And what's wrong with that may I ask?'

Sir Peter saw the relief in Maguire-Barton's eyes at the change of direction of the interview. 'Mr Holloway is also a contact of Mr Grushko and has received certain benefits from him that would take a lot of explaining.'

'What kind of benefits?'

'Much the same as you received yourself from the same source. All-expenses-paid trips to Warsaw Pact capitals for instance.'

'I was a member of a parliamentary group.'

'You've had four trips to Prague, one to Warsaw, two to Sofia and two to Moscow which were all private trips. And on at least three of those trips you used a passport that was not your own.'

'Whose passport was it?'

'That would be given in evidence if the matter came before a court. It's hard evidence, on the record.'

Maguire-Barton frowned. 'What court case are you on about?'

'Mr Maguire-Barton, you don't seem to appreciate that you might well be prosecuted for endangering the security of the State.'

'But that's preposterous.'

Now that it had got to the bluster and indignation stage Sir Peter had had enough.

'Preposterous or not, that is what will inevitably happen if you don't heed my advice.'

147

'What advice, for Christ's sake, I haven't had any advice.'

'I'm about to give you my advice, Maguire-Barton. It would be to your benefit if you not only listened, but listened carefully.'

'Don't sermonise – just say what you've got to say.'

For long moments Sir Peter looked at Maguire-Barton without speaking and he was aware of the white knuckles and the small vein that had come up on Maguire-Barton's forehead.

'I'm not sure in the light of your attitude that I want to give you advice. Maybe you'll learn quicker the hard way.'

'OK,' Maguire-Barton said quietly. 'Tell me what you want.'

'First of all I want you to understand that a record of our discussion will go on the files. I told you that this meeting had its formalities. That's one of them.' He paused. 'My advice is quite simple, Maguire-Barton. Stop playing games with Moscow. No more contacts with them, official or unofficial. And stop assisting or advising the people or groups who are trying to infiltrate your own Party.'

Maguire-Barton shrugged. 'And what if I don't go along with your advice?'

'Then we'll throw the book at you.'

'You haven't got a shred of evidence that a court would accept.'

'I won't comment on that piece of wishful thinking but you might care to reflect on what your position will be in the Party and outside when what we have is pinned on you in open court.'

'Are you threatening me?'

'Yes.'

'In that case . . .'

Sir Peter held up his hand. 'Don't go on, Maguire-Barton. I've had enough of you. But I warn you. One wrong move and your feet won't touch, you'll be at the Old Bailey before you can draw breath. And whether

148

you're found guilty or not you'll be finished, in public life and in private too.'

'You bastards should be controlled and I'll bloody well see that you are.'

Sir Peter stood up and said quietly, 'Don't tempt me, Maguire-Barton. You've had your little fling. Don't push your luck.' He walked to the desk and pressed one of the buttons on a panel. One of the juniors came in almost immediately.

'Jonathan, please show Mr Maguire-Barton the way out.' He turned to Maguire-Barton and said, 'Thank you so much for your co-operation Mr Maguire-Barton. You've been a great help.'

Maguire-Barton opened his mouth to speak, saw the look on Sir Peter's face, and then changed his mind, heading for the open door.

26

Macleod and Shapiro had always got on well despite the rifts that sometimes disturbed the various levels of relationships between SIS and the CIA. Macleod was in his middle-fifties, experienced, a good negotiator and always amiable and relaxed. And always used the opportunity of the liaison meeting to get Shapiro's views on current CIA problems concerning the KGB. On several occasions tentative offers had been made to the Brit to recruit him to the CIA. But Shapiro knew that his almost unlimited brief on combating the KGB in SIS would not be possible in the much larger organisation in the USA. In London he was three thousand miles nearer the Soviet Union. They were almost at the end of the agenda of their routine Washington liaison meeting when Macleod raised the point under 'Any other business.'

He looked at Shapiro. 'Have you got any points?'

'Nothing official.'

'What unofficial?'

'There was a question raised at my last liaison meeting with GCHQ. They queried whether Fort George Meade ever passed on commercial surveillance material to US companies that could disadvantage British industry or commerce.'

'What did you say to them?'

'I assured them that it didn't happen and would never happen but I promised to raise the point either with NSA or you guys on a semi-official basis.'

'Well let's put the cards on the table. The National Security Agency, as you know, carries out radio and telephonic surveillance on everything. Specific targets are the main traffic but their listening facilities are non-specific. They sweep the whole world like a damn great vacuum cleaner and suck in everything. Radio at all levels, satellites, telephones – the lot. And that includes commercial stuff. Foreign and domestic. Indiscriminately. The censorship comes at evaluation level.

'There's no way we can handle all we get but some commercial stuff has a security element in it. High-tech and weaponry for instance. Also the movement of large sums of cash here and overseas. That stuff's pulled out with check-words. The rest is retained on tape for two months and then wiped clean. It's treated as highly confidential before it's destroyed and that's because we recognise that that information could make a guy a fortune or even destroy an industry.' He paused. 'So we care, Joe, we really do. If it was leaked, which would be very difficult because of our cut-out systems, we should treat it internally as a criminal offence and any outsiders involved would be treated the same.'

'Have you ever uncovered a leak, Robert?'

'Yes. Two. Both way back. They were picked up in hours. The NSA employee concerned has spent the last two years manning a dish aerial on some lonely rock in the Pacific, and the guy who suborned him never quite worked out how his company went bust inside six months. In the second case we intercepted the whole deal at an early stage and the information passed on was both spurious and damaging to the company that received it. The NSA person concerned not only was dismissed without a reference but never quite understood why she was called in by the IRS to look at her tax returns for the previous eight years. It cost her seventeen thousand bucks.' He shrugged. 'So that's the picture. Cards on the table. Not even the President could ask for that stuff without authentication of grounds. It's dynamite and we know it. OK?'

'I'll pass it on. But I guess they'll raise it again from time to time. Any points from you?'

Macleod smiled. 'Yes. Same sort of query. Our Polish and Soviet people think you've been holding back on them in the last few months.'

'What grounds do they give?'

Macleod pulled out a slip of paper from the inside pocket of his jacket and read it before he looked back at Shapiro.

'They say that the exchange of information shows a very obvious deterioration. Routine stuff, OK, but your usual top-level stuff has been missing. Seems they set great value on that information.'

'How great a value?'

'My impression was that they consider that that "special source" material is vital.'

'They're right in saying that. It's dried up I'm afraid.'

'They told me that they've put a lot of cash and effort into supporting that operation. They're not pleased. I need to give them a convincing explanation or I think it can mean a high-level hassle. Way above you and me. And the possible withdrawal of reciprocal information.'

'The explanation's simple, Jake. Our man disappeared some months back. We assume that he's in the bag.'

'Oh. I'm sorry to hear that. Why weren't we told?'

'Because we don't know what's happened. He may not have been picked up. He boarded a scheduled domestic flight from Warsaw to Moscow. The plane never landed at Sheremetyevo. We've cast around a bit but we've drawn a complete blank and we don't want to indicate an interest that would blow his cover if it isn't already blown.'

'Can I tell my people this?'

'We'd rather you didn't.'

'Why? Don't you trust our people?'

'We just don't want to stir the pool. He may be in the Lubyanka but not talking. He may be dead. He may have been involved in an air-crash that they have never publicised.'

'We've got people in both Warsaw and Moscow who could keep their ears to the ground if they knew more.'

Shapiro shrugged but didn't reply, and Macleod said, 'Would you talk to my guys?'

'If London clear it – yes.'

Macleod pointed to the red phone on his desk. 'Call 'em, Joe. I'll leave you alone.' He smiled. 'It's auto-scrambler. And it's not monitored.'

Shapiro talked with London for nearly an hour and it was only his suggestion that if they came clean with the CIA they might co-operate on an exchange that made London agree to him going ahead. A meeting was arranged by Macleod for the following day in Washington.

Macleod walked with Shapiro from his hotel to the meeting in the private house in Foggy Bottom. It was a modest town house on 24th Street not far from Washington Circle. There was a small, neat front-garden and a white picket fence and a paved pathway that led to the front door.

Macleod made the introductions and Shapiro noticed that he only introduced two of the three men. The third had nodded and half-smiled but had not been named or introduced.

Goldsmith and Merrick were typical of the broad spectrum of American society from which the CIA recruited its officers. Goldsmith was tall and lean and in his early fifties. He had taught history at Berkeley, specialising in the history of revolution. Merrick was in his thirties, heavily built and already showing a tendency to pudginess, but he had a sharp mind and a forceful personality. Son of a California fruit farmer he had surprised his contemporaries by his success at Yale. And surprised them even more when he was invited to join a well-established law firm in Washington. When he had successfully represented various interests of the CIA he had been recruited, not as a legal adviser, but as a clear-minded situation evaluator.

They listened attentively to Shapiro's report on the disappearance of Phoenix. He had not been entirely candid about all the operation, particularly in its early

153

days, and he had said nothing that would enable them or their colleagues in Warsaw to pinpoint Phoenix's identity or official position in the Polish security service. When he finished it was Merrick who started the questions.

'This guy, Phoenix, how good was his Russian?'

'At least as good as his English. He was bi-lingual and Russian was his first language.'

'And his Polish?'

'Fluent but not perfect.'

Goldsmith said, 'Have you considered that he may have gone over – defected?'

'Of course.'

'And your evaluation?'

'Unlikely to the point of not worth considering seriously.'

'And how likely is it that he would talk under pressure?'

Shapiro shrugged. 'Who can tell? He had the usual training but our experience is that you can never tell until it happens. Sometimes it's the tough macho who's spilling the beans after ten minutes and your ivory tower intellectual who goes silent to the Gulag.'

'If you had to bet, which way would it go?'

'Not talking.'

Goldsmith looked at Shapiro. 'Was he the source of the material we got on the inside of the KGB HQ?'

'Yes.'

'And on the Polish Politburo?'

'It's fair to say that any top-level inside stuff concerning the Warsaw government and the KGB came from Phoenix.'

Merrick nodded. 'Could you give us a brief picture of his activities?' When he saw Shapiro hesitate he went on, 'You can rely on anything you say staying inside this room, Joe. We appreciate how delicate the situation is for you people.'

Shapiro looked away for a moment towards the window and then down at his clasped hands on the table. Then he raised his head and looked at Merrick.

154

'He spoke English, and fluent Russian and Polish. He was recruited by SIS from the Army. He was intensively trained to go back to Poland and infiltrate into any government establishment that could give us an inside picture of what was going on inside the regime.

'For five years he has been Deputy Chief Liaison Officer between Polish Intelligence and the KGB in Warsaw and Moscow. He fed us information on the Soviet internal rivalries, the organisation and personnel of the KGB in Moscow and Warsaw, especially those who were active against Britain and the United States.

'He prevented both Langley and London from making several major mistakes in our operations and it's fair to say that there was little that they planned against either of us that we were not warned about. Not always in precise detail but enough to allow us to take general precautions.'

Macleod intervened, looking at his two colleagues. 'The Agency's considered comment to me was that the material provided by SIS from this agent was the only reliable material that we have received in the last four years. I understand that it is the wish of the Director himself that we furnish any help we can to assist SIS.'

Goldsmith said softly, 'What help do they need that we can provide?'

Shapiro shrugged. 'There is nothing that could help us at the moment. The reason why Robert Macleod wanted this meeting was so that I could clear up your doubts that we were deliberately holding back information from you. I hope I have convinced you on that score.' He paused. 'But if I could move to the future for a moment – maybe our friends in CIA *could* help. I'm hypothesising that we discover that Pheonix has been taken. Whether he's talked or not doesn't really matter. We should want to get him out. We have nobody of theirs at the moment who would make the Soviets interested in an exchange. If we put all our Warsaw Pact prisoners together Moscow wouldn't be interested for a moment.' Shapiro paused again. 'Have you got anybody?'

155

Goldsmith and Merrick looked at Macleod, who looked across at the man who had not been introduced and who had contributed nothing to the conversation. He in turn looked at Shapiro for several moments before he spoke.

He said very quietly, 'My name's Paul Nowak. I'm also CIA. We don't have anybody who would constitute a likely exchange for Phoenix.'

Shapiro nodded. 'Can I ask you why you are here at this meeting, Mr Nowak?'

'I'm just an observer.'

'Why is that necessary? Does somebody not trust your colleagues here?'

'I don't have to give a reason.'

'Only three or four people in Britain know about Phoenix. I've talked to your colleagues as a courtesy, I don't appreciate having somebody else in the picture without it being established that they have a need to know. A man's life is at stake.'

'I came because I was invited to come. It's not just curiosity I assure you.'

Shapiro looked at Macleod who looked across at Nowak. 'I trust Joe Shapiro implicitly, Paul. So does the Director. Are you going to tell him or shall I?'

Nowak stood up and walked to the door. Before he opened it he looked at Macleod. 'I won't tell him. If you do . . .' He shrugged, '. . . then it's your responsibility.'

Macleod nodded, his face calm and showing no concern at the apparent threat. When Nowak had left, Macleod said, 'Nowak's under a lot of stress at the moment. I won't go into the details.' He paused. 'What matters is that what he said is quite correct. At the moment we have no suitable body for exchange. But it is possible that that could change in the next couple of months.'

'Can I be told the basics?'

'OK. But just the basics. We have a man in custody. An important Soviet. He'll be coming to the final stages of the legal battle in the next few weeks. Nowak was in charge of the operation. There may be a legal cock-up.

156

Nowak is obsessed by getting him the death sentence or at least life. When it all eventually gets untangled there's just the possibility that the best solution would be an exchange. Nowak knows this but doesn't want to admit it so that an exchange doesn't become an alternative in the legal people's minds and they hold back from making a one hundred per cent effort to nail the guy.'

'Is this Sivrin at the UN, or is it Colonel Abel?'

Macleod shook his head. 'I can't answer any more questions, Joe. But it's not Sivrin.'

'Can I keep in touch with you on this?'

'By all means. But remember – it's vague on both sides. On your side you don't even know that you need an exchange. And on our side we don't know if it's a possibility.'

'Is your guy in the same league as Phoenix?'

'Maybe higher. Even more important. We think. Do you want me to book you a flight? I'll take you to the airport myself.'

'That would be fine, Robert.'

27

The trial of Lonsdale and his network was set for March 13, 1961, only narrowly depriving the press of the chance to quote Shakespeare and the Ides of March. By then the media knew quite a lot about the private lives of the accused but nothing of their alleged activities. The original formal charge gave no details. But they had to restrain their eagerness to unveil glowing statements from Lonsdale's discarded girlfriends, the love-life of Houghton and Gee and the middle-class normality of the Krogers. It was all *sub judice* until the verdict had been given.

So the personal stories were of the barristers who were to prosecute or defend. The Attorney-General, Sir Reginald Manningham-Buller, headed the prosecution, and four leading counsel were to appear for the defence, one each for Houghton, Gee, the Krogers and Lonsdale.

Sir Reginald was already quite well known to the public. Bespectacled, fifty-five, testy in public but kindly and witty in private, he had a reputation for crushing his opponents like a legalistic steamroller. Living in the market town of Towcester, he was inevitably pictured as a man of the rolling acres despite the fact that his house and gardens barely made up to six acres. Word pictures were painted in the Sunday press before the trial of Sir Reginald pruning his floribunda roses to soothe his nerves before rising in court next day for what seemed to be Britain's most important spy-trial.

Baron Parker of Waddington, the Lord Chief Justice, was to preside at the trial. A gentle, moderate and modest man. Against the death penalty, but for corporal punishment. A man who had had to give up his rare hobby on appointment as Lord Chief Justice. The study of genetics applied to the breeding of high butter-fat dairy cattle.

The barrister defending Lonsdale was the grandson of an admiral and the son of a naval officer killed in the war. Born in Guernsey in the Channel Islands Mr W.M.F. Hudson was well aware of the significance of the charges against his client.

Two barristers from the same chambers were to defend Houghton and Gee. Mr Henry Palmer was to defend Houghton, and his equally young colleague Mr James Dunlop was to defend Gee.

The heavyweight of the defence team was Mr Victor Durand QC, a tough, able barrister who was to defend Peter and Helen Kroger.

When the trial started the defence objected to twelve of the jurors. Nine men and three women. It was finally an all-male jury.

Lonsdale sat in the dock, smartly dressed in a light grey suit. Ethel Gee wore a dark blue dress and Helen Kroger wore a heather mixture costume.

The Attorney-General opened the case, describing the circumstances of the arrests and of the accused and the details of what had been discovered in the parcel handed by Ethel Gee to Lonsdale. And then he went meticulously through the espionage material found at Lonsdale's flat, the farm cottage, Houghton's home and the Krogers' bungalow.

It became obvious that the Krogers' bungalow was the hub of the network. The searchers had found a microscope that could be used for reading micro-dots, a list of radio call-signs using the names of Russian rivers, a high-powered radio transmitter hidden under a trapdoor in the kitchen, one-time code pads and several letters in Russian. There were two New Zealand passports in the Krogers' names, a Ronson table lighter with a concealed cavity in its base which contained film; the camera that had been in Lonsdale's briefcase deposited in the Midland Bank was in the study.

The Attorney-General showed the jury a tin of well-known talcum powder which had a special compartment with a standard KGB micro-dot reader. There were black-painted boards in the loft to cover the bathroom windows so that the bathroom could be used for enlarging or reducing photographed material. Also in the loft was 74 feet of aerial which led to a radiogram in the sitting room. Under the loft insulation were several thousand US dollars, and American and British travellers' cheques.

At Houghton's semi-detached cottage was a list of the Admiralty Test pamphlets that had been passed to Lonsdale. Further Test pamphlets were found hidden in Houghton's radiogram. There were Admiralty charts with pencil markings of secret submarine exercise areas, others had pencil marks pinpointing the site of suitable pieces of equipment for sabotage. £500 in Premium Bonds and a camera were found in a drawer with what looked like a box of normal Swan matches. Under the base of the match-box was a paper which registered dates for meetings and codes if a meeting had to be called off. In an empty tin of Snowcem paint in a garden shed was £650 in pound and ten shilling notes.

In Lonsdale's flat there was another Ronson lighter with a concealed cavity holding radio signal plans similar to those found at the Krogers' place. There was a similar tin of talcum powder with its hidden micro-dot reader, and a large amount of money in US dollars and sterling.

Nowak listened with envy as the prosecution established the evidence and its significance in carrying out espionage. The Attorney-General established the connections between them that constituted a conspiracy. Compared with the legal circus that they had had to go through in New York it all looked so simple..

Witnesses gave evidence of how the various espionage items were used and others gave details of dates, times and locations of meetings.

160

Houghton had offered to turn Queen's Evidence against the other four if the charges against him could be dropped but the prosecution had refused the offer. They were confident that they didn't need his testimony.

A Special Branch officer explained how the false passport had been obtained but there was no way that the prosecution could prove that Lonsdale was a Russian. They read out letters translated from Russian that were from a woman named Galyusha who wrote as if she were his wife. But the jury, the court, and the general public got the message, and the prosecution would have gained little even if they had been able to prove that he was Russian.

On the second day of the trial the Attorney-General established in considerable detail the evidence that had only been touched on in the first day, and defence counsel queried as best they could the significance and accuracy of the evidence given by witnesses whose names were not given for security reasons.

Some embarrassment to the security services arose on the third day when a witness who had been instructed by a solicitor to sort through the possessions of the Krogers at their bungalow in Cranley Drive gave his evidence. Despite the previous searches by Special Branch, the witness had discovered two passports concealed in the cover and lining of a writing case. The witness had also discovered $4,000 concealed in a pair of book-ends.

A specialist naval officer gave evidence that the transmitter found in the Krogers' house was amply capable of transmitting to Moscow and beyond. A Russian-language expert confirmed that the signal schedules found in the Krogers' Ronson lighter and the lighter from Lonsdale's flat were similar, and included coded transmission details under the headings 'transmission blind' and 'transmissions on orders of centre'.

The next day included the evidence of a communications expert from the HQ of the British monitoring services. Using the signals plan found in the Krogers' bungalow he

161

had plotted the bearings and confirmed that the transmitter covered was sited in Moscow.

Towards the end of the day the defence began calling witnesses. When the trial resumed on the following Monday most of the court's time was taken up with defence counsel's attempt to establish that Houghton had acted only under threat and that Gee had been a reluctant partner.

By the Wednesday it was the Krogers' turn. Their several changes of name were touched on. The Attorney-General also brought out their connection with the Rosenbergs in the USA and their connections with Colonel Abel.

On Wednesday March 22, 1961 the Lord Chief Justice said of Lonsdale: 'You are clearly a professional spy. It is a dangerous career and one in which you must be prepared – and no doubt *are* prepared – to suffer if you are caught.'

He passed sentence of 25 years' imprisonment.

Of the Krogers he said: 'I cannot distinguish between either of you – you are both in this up to the hilt. You are both professional spies.'

They received sentences of 20 years each.

Houghton and Gee were both given sentences of 15 years and Lord Parker condemned them as traitors to their country whose motive was sheer greed.

With the trial over the press gave itself up to an orgy of revelation. Houghton's ex-wife described a marriage of physical cruelty and meanness. Lonsdale's ex-girlfriends and mistresses described in vivid detail his charm and generosity and hinted that his prowess as a lover was incredible. Those who studied the simian features of Lonsdale's photographs wondered if that mean-eyed face was really that of the man the women had described. A couple of newspapers mounted the usual campaign that the secret service was inefficient and a few MPs called for an enquiry.

Media interest in the case was short-lived. The new E-type Jaguar was more interesting at £1,480 plus purchase tax and it still wasn't easy to get tickets for *My Fair Lady* at Drury Lane.

162

28

The house in Georgetown had been converted from a derelict warehouse with great skill and taste. Two teams of CIA electronics engineers had swept it thoroughly and declared it clean. It was used as a safe-house by the CIA for top-secret meetings. As added security, there were no telephones. Communication with the outside world was by messenger or radio.

Six places had been arranged around a glass-topped table for the meeting, but there were none of the usual scrap-pads or writing materials that went with normal meetings for note-taking. It had been agreed beforehand that there would be no record of the meeting.

The three Americans chatted about the weather, the new CIA pay-scales and their views on Allen Drury's *Advise and Consent*, anything except the matter that had brought them there.

When the two Britishers arrived, Shapiro from SIS and Andrews from CIA-SIS liaison, there were handshakes all round and introductions to the two Americans they had not already met.

It was Macleod who started them off, smiling as he pushed an ash-tray towards Andrews.

'Apologies for the formal arrangements.' He laughed. 'Unfortunately, we don't have furniture for a more informal layout.' He paused. 'However, we all know why we are here and we all know that this meeting is informal and off-the-record.' He nodded towards Shapiro. 'I'll leave it to Mr Shapiro to start the ball rolling.'

Shapiro took a deep breath. 'As you know, I've come to ask for help from the CIA.' He looked at the three Americans' faces but there was no response. 'For many years we have passed on to the CIA almost all the information from one of our top agents. I think it's fair to say that most of the CIA's information on both the internal politics of the KGB and Polish intelligence came solely from this source. I'm authorised to tell you now that the man concerned was in fact the liaison officer between the Polish security service and the KGB. But he is actually an Englishman.' Shapiro paused and looked around the table. 'You can imagine the courage it took to maintain that cover. And you can imagine the importance to both SIS and CIA of having that level of information.' He paused and then said quietly, 'At the moment that man is in a special punishment section of a Gulag labour-camp. Perhaps I should add that he is a commissioned officer in the Intelligence Corps with the rank of captain. We understand from two sources that he has been very badly treated and is unlikely to survive more than three or four months.' Shapiro paused again. 'We have nobody of similar importance to offer as an exchange. I should like to ask officially – if you would consider offering Moscow an exchange for this officer.' Shapiro took a deep breath. 'Maybe I ought to declare an interest. I recruited this man myself. We had a very special relationship. I explained the risks but he went ahead willingly.' He paused and his voice quavered slightly as he said softly, 'I feel personally responsible for his terrible situation.'

For several moments there was silence around the table and then Macleod said, 'Have you any indication that Moscow would agree to such an exchange?'

'We have nothing comparable to offer so we haven't made any approach, either unofficial or official.'

Macleod said quietly, 'What made you come to us at this particular moment?'

Shapiro shrugged. 'Two reasons only. Firstly because you've got Abel, and secondly we only heard two days ago that our man was alive and in the Kolyma Gulag.'

'Did you know that Abel and Gary Powers's parents are trying to persuade Moscow to do an exchange for Gary Powers, the U-2 pilot?'

'Yes I knew that from your weekly sitrep.'

Da Costa chipped in. 'You're asking us to leave one of our own citizens in a Soviet prison for the sake of your own man.'

'He was hardly our *own* man. He was virtually working for you as well. He was under our control but you got almost everything that we got.'

Macleod turned to look at da Costa. 'We contributed funds to this operation, Ray. And it wasn't just a hand-out. It was on the Director's instructions.'

Nowak said, 'There are already rumours in the press about an exchange for Powers. There'd be hell to pay if we ended up leaving Powers to rot in the Lubyanka and brought back a Brit instead.'

Macleod looked at Shapiro. 'What do you say to that?'

'It's undoubtedly a problem.' For a moment he looked uncomfortable. 'I don't like saying this but isn't our man more important than Gary Powers?'

Da Costa half-smiled. 'D'you mean more important or more deserving?'

Shapiro shrugged. 'I wouldn't dream of passing any comment about what your guy deserves. I just claim that our man is worth exchanging for anybody we've got. Either of us.'

'Why don't you offer them Lonsdale?'

'We're quite prepared to do that but we don't think that they set as much value on him as they do on Abel. And they'd certainly want the Krogers as well. The couple who worked for Abel in New York – the Cohens.'

Da Costa said quietly, 'So why don't you try them first and maybe have Abel as a fall-back position. If our people agreed.'

165

'We've had indications that there's a batting order of people who Moscow want and Lonsdale is at best about third on the list. Maybe not even that high.'

'And Abel is number one in your opinion?'

'No. Abel is number two on their list.'

'So who's their number one?'

'The defector. Hayhanen.'

There was a chorus of protest but Macleod held up a silencing hand as he looked at his colleagues. 'Nobody's suggesting that we trade Hayhanen, but Joe Shapiro's right in his assessment.' He turned to look at Shapiro. 'What is it you want us to go with?'

'A flat refusal on Hayhanen. Try offering Lonsdale – with the Krogers thrown in if necessary. And if that doesn't work I'd like to be able to offer Abel, as a last resort.'

There was a long silence and then Macleod said, 'How about we break for half an hour and I'll walk around the block with Joe while you guys think about it?'

Nobody dissented and as they walked slowly round the block Shapiro said, 'Are your people in a mood to help, Robert?'

'Well, they're on your side, that's for sure. It's the problem of leaving Powers to rot that worries them. The public won't like that. They won't understand. And none of us – FBI and CIA – is anybody's favourite son at the moment.'

'I think there is a solution that could avoid any problem about Gary Powers.'

'You're a cunning old fox, Joe Shapiro. You'd better tell them what you've got in mind.'

When they got back to the house the others settled back round the table and Macleod said, 'Joe's got some thoughts on this situation.' He paused and looked at Shapiro. 'Tell us what you've got in mind, Joe.'

Joe looked around the table at each of them. 'Let me tell you first how I think those guys in Dzerzhinski Square will be thinking.

'Their guy Abel is a sick man according to what I've heard. A disappointed man too. Disappointed that Moscow haven't raised a finger so far to get him released. He was their top guy in New York – maybe in the States for that matter. And he'll have expected that they'd at least try for a deal. But they ain't tried – have they?

'So when they're forced to consider a deal about him they'll know that we'll have tipped him off that we're offering Moscow a deal. If they refuse they'll know that he'll be a very bitter man. He's kept silent so far – and they'll know that too. But if they refuse a deal then maybe his attitude would change. He's had some years in prison but he won't ever have contemplated actually spending the last years of his life in jail. Dying in jail. The KGB will assume that if he was left to rot by them he could well feel that he's done his bit and with a nice offer from you guys he might jump at the chance of co-operating. If Moscow don't care about him why should he tough it out?

'Now we come to our guy – code-name Phoenix. He won't ever talk – no matter what they do to him – no matter what they offer him. I've had word that he's a very sick man. Physically and mentally. They've put him through the mincing machine, that's for sure.' He shrugged. 'He's of no use to them and they will know it.'

As he paused da Costa interrupted. 'That sounds like a stand-off, Joe.'

Shapiro shook his head. 'No. It's not. There's two things to bear in mind. Firstly, Abel will know he's going to spend the rest of his life in jail. Abel has hopes, our man has none.' He paused. 'There's one other plus factor on our side. The Russians have never publicised the capture of our man – no show-trial for the world's press – the usual scenario. Why?'

Macleod said softly, 'They don't want to lose face. They don't want the world to know they were fooled by your man. That a top KGB liaison man with the Poles was a mole for the West.'

167

Shapiro nodded. 'And they wouldn't dare put him on show in court after they'd beaten him up and he still wasn't admitting to anything.'

Da Costa said, 'That still leaves the problem of Powers, Joe.'

Shapiro shook his head slowly. 'Powers isn't a problem. He's our ace in the hole.'

'How come?'

'We do the deal with Moscow so that as far as the rest of the world is concerned we exchange Abel for Powers. The deal for Phoenix is a secret deal. Never to be revealed by either side. And he doesn't come over at Check-point Charlie or any of the usual Berlin crossing points.'

Macleod nodded. 'And if the Russians say no?'

'We stick to our position. No deal for our guy means no deal for Abel.'

Nowak said, 'And what if Langley or the White House say "no"?'

'And you trade Abel just for Powers?'

'Yep.'

Shapiro pursed his lips reflectively. 'Well, apart from the whole of the Western world thinking you were either very naive or very weak to trade a top Soviet spy for a run-of-the-mill pilot, I'd say you would be wise to reflect on what effect it would have on your relationship with SIS.'

Da Costa said quickly, 'Are you talking with official backing when you say that, Joe?'

'Not at all. I'm not even suggesting that it would be official government policy or even official SIS policy. But a lot of top people in SIS would have very hard feelings about working with CIA or the FBI in future.'

Da Costa said, 'That's blackmail, Joe.'

Shapiro shook his head vigorously. 'It's not, Mr da Costa. And let me assure you that if I thought that blackmail was the only way then I'd resort to blackmail. All I'm asking for is help and consideration from my colleagues. You people.'

168

Macleod raised his eyebrows. 'It's rather more than help and consideration, Joe.'

'It's very urgent, Robbie. Desperately urgent. I need a quick reaction.'

Macleod nodded and looked at the others. 'I'll take our friends back to their hotel. I'll be back in about an hour. Kick it around while I'm away.'

Da Costa stood up. 'Before you go, what's your view, Robbie?'

'I go for it. But with a proviso. It has to be approved by State and the Director CIA.' Macleod turned to the two Britishers. 'Let's go.'

When Macleod and the Englishmen had gone da Costa walked over to the window. For a few minutes he stood there and then turned to look at Nowak.

'What d'you think?'

'You're against it, aren't you?'

'Not really. But I don't think it'll work.'

'Why not?'

'I don't think the KGB will play ball. Not two for one.'

'They've had all they want out of Powers. A trial, a public confrontation, an abject apology for being a naughty boy. What more can they get out of him? And the world won't know it's two for one.'

'It'll take weeks to negotiate. According to what Shapiro said their chap could be dead by then.'

'All the more reason for the Russians to get their fingers out.'

'And we give up any chance we've got of getting Abel to come over to us and spill the beans.'

'He won't come over. They've tried everything they know. He just smiles and shakes his head. He's built up this image of himself now. The friendly, intelligent and patriotic soldier who bears his punishment with dignity and courage. He'd never abandon that for being a defector.'

'What will the brass say d'you reckon?'

169

'The Director CIA will say "yes". The Secretary of State will say "no".'

'And then ?'

'It'll be up to the President. I'd guess he'll say "yes".'

Late the same evening Macleod drove Shapiro out to CIA HQ at Langley and they sat in a small office with a microfiche reader and a small bundle of fiches, marking the CIA references of typical material that had come from Phoenix.

It was 4 a.m. when they finished and a secretary had typed up the list. The information concerned had been collated onto two fiches while Macleod and Shapiro slept in a couple of small duty officers' bunks. Macleod woke Shapiro at 8 a.m. with shaving kit and talked to him as he washed and shaved.

As Nowak had forecast, the response from the CIA Director had been positive, and from the State Department negative. The President would make the decision. He would be at his desk by 8.30, would sample the information on the fiches and make his decision. He might ask to see Shapiro and ask some questions: Macleod was to put the facts to the President verbally.

It was 11 a.m. when Macleod returned. The President had agreed after seeing the representative samples of the kind of information that Phoenix had been supplying. He had even wished them luck and had asked to be kept informed.

29

Although Nowak had been so determined to get a conviction against Colonel Abel he was aware that the prosecution had sailed very near the wind to get that conviction. And he was aware too that they had not been able to establish even one actual act of espionage against the Russian. Now it was all over he felt a sneaking respect for the man who had refused to talk or co-operate in any way, and he was pleased to be the bearer of good news.

He sat at the plain wooden table in the prison office block waiting for the Russian to be shown in. A week-old copy of *Pravda* which he had brought with him lay on the table alongside a carton of Marlboros. When he heard the footsteps in the corridor outside he stood up and faced the door. He was shocked by the Russian's appearance. He was much thinner, his clothes hanging loose on his gaunt frame and his steps unsteady. He waved the old man to the chair and sat down facing him.

'I've got some good news for you, Colonel.'

The old man nodded but said nothing.

'We're trying to negotiate an exchange with Moscow. You for one of our own men.'

When Abel still made no reply Nowak said, 'Are you OK, Colonel? Are you feeling all right?'

The old man looked at the American. 'I saw a few reports of this in the newspapers some weeks ago.' He half smiled. 'The young pilot was mentioned. A Mr Powers, yes?'

'Yes.'

The old man shrugged. 'I didn't believe it. I still don't believe it.'

'Why not?'

The Russian pursed his lips. 'Experience. Experience of Moscow and experience of Washington. It's a piece of propaganda.'

'How do you make that out?'

'Moscow have made no move to suggest an exchange. Why should they? I have kept silent. And I shall remain silent. So what do they gain?'

'That's a bit cynical isn't it?'

'Not cynical. Just realistic.'

'And Washington?'

The old man sighed. 'You think after all the trouble you people went to to have me convicted that they're going to trade me for a pilot who embarrassed you all, from Eisenhower down?' He shook his head. 'No way, my friend, no way.'

Nowak smiled. 'I think you're going to be surprised, Colonel.'

'No, sir. It's you people who are going to be surprised.'

'How come?'

'Because I won't agree to the exchange myself.'

Abel saw the shock and surprise on the American's face and despised him for his naivety.

'And one more thing, my friend. The pieces in the newspapers. The pleading by the pilot's parents are propaganda too. One more stick to beat the Soviets with. The hard-hearted men in the Kremlin.' He shook his head. 'You won't get me to join in the charade.'

'I swear to you – there's no charade. It's a genuine attempt to release you and Gary Powers.'

'Whatever it is – count me out. I shall not co-operate.'

'You don't have any choice, Colonel,' Nowak said quietly.

Abel smiled coldly. 'Even your own media will condemn you and the European press will have a field day. The

172

American State Department sending back a Russian who asks for asylum.'

'You mean you would actually do that?'

'You can rely on it, my friend.'

'But why?'

'Think about it. Work it out very carefully. And remember what we tell our new KGB recruits: when you've looked at every possibility and it still won't fit – then try the impossibilities.' Abel stood up. 'I'd like to go back to my cell.'

Shapiro and Macleod were sitting in the VIP lounge at the airport when the girl came over to say that Macleod was wanted on the phone. He was away for about ten minutes and when he came back he told Shapiro of Nowak's meeting with Abel.

'Would you people let me talk to him?'

'Why? Do you think you could make him change his mind?'

'I'd like the chance to try.'

'We'd better tell the desk that you're not taking this flight.'

Back at the CIA's HQ at Langley, Shapiro hung around trying to hide his tension as Macleod consulted his colleagues. It was almost an hour before Macleod came back.

It had been agreed that he could interview Abel, but it was obvious that it had been a reluctant agreement. It was conditional on him not mentioning or even hinting at the inclusion of Phoenix in the proposed exchange. He would be flown to the Atlanta Penitentiary by military plane the next day. Nowak would go with him but they had agreed that he could see Abel alone.

A local CIA officer had driven them to the prison and Nowak had introduced Shapiro to the Prison Warden and then left him.

173

'He's got a cell of his own, Mr Shapiro. You could talk to him there or in the visitors' room. You'd be alone in either place.'

'Would you have any objections to me talking to him in the open air, the recreation area maybe?'

'Can I ask you why?'

Shapiro sighed. 'You know his background, Warden. He'll take it for granted that any inside place is bugged. I'd like him to feel free to talk. It could be important.'

'We've got a sports area. You could talk to him there. He's not violent and he's a bit too old and too rational to try and escape. How long do you think you'll need?'

'About a couple of hours maybe.'

'I'll get one of my men to take you there and somebody will bring him out to you.'

'Thanks for your co-operation.'

'You're welcome.'

Shapiro sat on a wooden bench at the far side of the sports field and took off his jacket as the sun beat down. He had tried to make notes the previous evening of what he would say to the KGB colonel but there was nothing to write down. He had no idea of what he should say. And why should the Russian be more influenced by talking to him rather than Nowak? But the thought of the man in the Gulag camp haunted him. He had had no peace of mind from the first moment when he learned that Phoenix was missing. It was as if history was repeating itself. Then he saw a uniformed prison officer open the wire-mesh door at the far end of the sports field. Shapiro watched as the tall lean figure of the man in the outsize suit came through the open gate. He was almost a hundred yards away. It wasn't until he was twenty feet away that Abel recognised the man who was sitting on the bench.

30

Sir Peter Clark's cottage was on the outskirts of Petersfield. Its grounds were no more than one acre but they gave onto the village cricket ground which in turn sloped upwards to a wooded hillside lined with beech and oak. Shapiro and Morton had been waved to wicker armchairs with cushions while Sir Peter sat on a rustic bench that was green with age and weathering. In an odd way their chosen drinks expressed much of their individual characters. Shapiro was drinking whisky, Morton locally brewed beer and Sir Peter was sipping from a glass of milk.

'Tell me again, Joe. It was before my time. Why did you think . . .' He paused, sensing that he was beginning to build a sentence that implied either blame or criticism, '. . . remind me of the circumstances.'

Morton, sensing Shapiro's confusion, said, 'We had to make sure that the minimum number of people knew of what was planned. The only people involved in the decision were Joe, myself and Sir Mortimer who was D-G at that time. And even he was told only of the general outline. We gave him no details of names or background on the plan itself. All we were concerned with was that if things went wrong at some stage – and there was a political rumpus – at least he would be forewarned.'

'Did he tell the PM?'

'He didn't tell us. My belief is that he did.'

'And there was no come-back from him?'

'Not that we knew of.'

'Go on . . .' Sir Peter nodded towards Shapiro as he looked at Morton, '. . . let Joe speak for himself, Hughie. It's only between the three of us even now.'

'The Americans have made a big gesture, Sir Peter.' Shapiro shrugged. 'In appreciation of the past information that has come from Phoenix. They have authorised me to negotiate an exchange – Colonel Abel for Phoenix. But that exchange will be top-secret. So far as the public are concerned Abel will be exchanged for the U-2 pilot, Gary Powers. I'd like your authority to go ahead with this.'

Sir Peter looked towards the village cricket field, then at Morton, and finally at Shapiro.

'You've been almost obsessed about this problem of Phoenix, ever since the news first came through. Why, Joe?'

'Because I'm responsible for what has happened to him. I recruited him. I planned his training and his whole set-up. I owe it to him to do anything – anything – I can to get him back.'

'You explained to him the risks honestly and fairly?'

'Yes.'

'And you told him what we always tell undercover people, that we should not be able to help them if they were caught. That we should deny their existence and any knowledge of them?'

'Yes.'

'And this kind of situation has happened before. A dozen times even in my time as D-G, yes?'

'Yes.'

'And in half those cases we played it by the book and in time we got them back.'

'It took years in every case. The information we have is that Phoenix is seriously ill in Kolyma Camp. One of the worst of the Gulag camps. He'll just die there if we don't do something positive.'

'Do you feel even the smallest suspicion of guilt that you may not have really laid it on the line with Phoenix?'

'No. But I feel a hell of a lot of guilt that I recruited him in the first place.'

'You've recruited scores of men in your time, Joe. You always took it in your stride. Why this sudden concern for one man?'

Shapiro looked exasperated. 'I can't understand why this offer by the Americans isn't being grabbed with both hands.'

'Oh, but it is. You have my authority right now to go ahead in an attempt to negotiate an exchange. All that concerns me is that you seem to be rushing things. You're always so careful, so professional. I don't want you to risk making things worse than they already are.' He paused. 'And I'm concerned about you too.'

'In what way, Sir Peter?'

'We'll have a talk when this is over. Meantime – use any resources or help that you need. And the best of luck.'

When Shapiro had left, Morton said quietly, 'What's worrying you, Peter?'

Sir Peter shrugged. 'I don't know, Hughie. Just things that don't hang together properly.'

'Like what?'

'With hindsight it seems to me that when we decided to hand over the Lonsdale business to Five that Shapiro didn't mind. Normally he'd have fought like a tiger to keep it. I think that was because this Phoenix business was on his mind.' He looked at Morton for a moment. 'He went off to New York without mentioning what he had in mind – about the exchange I mean. Just gave the impression that it was a routine liaison meeting. That's not like Shapiro. I didn't say anything just now, but I didn't like it.'

'Anything else?'

'There's something that's changed Shapiro in the last few months. It reminds me of a report I saw on him when he was in Germany after the war. Said he was a loner and not suitable for high-level direction.'

'But that's exactly what he's been doing for the last ten

177

years – co-ordinating our activities against the KGB. And he's done it very well.'

'Remind me – how old is he?'

'This is his last year. He retires at the end of December.'

Sir Peter stood up, stretching his arms. 'I'll put him up for something in the New Year's list. Forget what I've been waffling about. It's probably me, not him, that's out of step.'

31

Max Lutz was the Berlin lawyer who always negotiated exchanges on behalf of the Soviet Union. He was in his early sixties. Wealthy, successful and sophisticated, he had acted for the Russians for twenty years. Apart from being a very successful lawyer he was a shrewd negotiator and had been a colonel in the Wehrmacht who had served in the Afrika Korps under Rommel, and later, in Europe, on the staff of Army Group 'B' under Field Marshal Modl.

One of the advantages of indirect negotiations had been that Lutz had established himself as an intermediary rather than a negotiator. This meant that bluffing and haggling were totally unacceptable. If either party turned down an original proposal then both parties were given one more opportunity to make a fresh proposal. If either party declined the second proposal the negotiations were over. There was no third chance. And Lutz would never participate in the future in any negotiation concerning any of the prisoners named in a rejected proposal. He maintained that men's freedom and lives were at stake and he would not be party to anything that could be construed as raising the hopes of a man or woman and their families and deliberately dashing these hopes. He was not a member of the Communist Party nor any other political party or group. He genuinely had no interest in politics. SIS has negotiated with Lutz half a dozen times over the years and respected the German's honesty and impartiality. Lutz was seldom told by either side the importance or otherwise, or the significance, of the prisoners concerned. They were names on a list and their priorities were not his concern. That was for their captors and countrymen to decide.

Two telephone calls to Berlin and a couple of days waiting and the call had come back setting up a meeting. The first meeting place was to be at Shapiro's hotel.

It was raining when Shapiro landed at Tegel. There was nobody to meet him and not even the head of station in Berlin had been informed of his visit. He took a taxi to Kempinski's and booked in under the name Macnay with a Canadian passport.

The desk phoned him an hour later. There was a Herr Lutz to see him. He asked them to send him up.

Herr Lutz was tall and thin and elegant. And he shook hands as if he really meant it before sitting down in the proffered armchair.

'So, Mr Macnay. A good journey, I hope.'

'Fine, thank you. Would you like a drink?'

'Maybe after we talk, yes. First business and then the schnapps.' He shrugged and smiled. 'As my countrymen always say, "Schnapps ist Schnapps und Arbeit ist Arbeit".'

'How do we start?'

'Perhaps you show me some identification first?'

Shapiro got up and walked over to the briefcase on the bed. He handed Lutz an SIS ID card and a letter that stated that he was authorised to discuss the possible exchange of prisoners on behalf of Washington and London.

Lutz studied them carefully and as he handed them back he reached in his pocket with his other hand and offered Shapiro a photostatted page which included his photograph and a statement in Russian, German and English that confirmed that he was authorised to discuss all matters concerning exchanges of prisoners with foreigners on behalf of Moscow. Lutz smiled as he slipped the paper back in his pocket.

'My clients in Moscow were surprised that you had contacted me.'

'Why is that?'

180

'They wonder who you have who is sufficiently important to warrant a meeting.'

Shapiro smiled. 'That sounds like the opening move of a professional negotiator decrying the other party's goods.'

Lutz looked shocked. 'I assure you, Mr Shapiro . . .' He smiled. 'I can call you Mr Shapiro I hope . . .' Lutz paused until Shapiro nodded and then went on. 'It is no such thing. There is no question of bargaining in these cases. If my clients are interested they will say so immediately. I assure you. We talk as intermediaries with the possibility of arranging something to both of our clients' mutual advantages.'

'So why are you surprised at our request for a meeting?'

'As you know, I am only called upon to act when the negotiations are . . . shall we say . . . concerning significant exchanges. There are other contacts and other systems for discussing the exchange of people of less significance.'

'So why the surprise?'

'Quite genuinely my clients know of nobody in your hands, either officially or unofficially, who they could classify as being of high significance.'

'I'm representing United States interests as well as British interests.'

'Ah, yes – of course.' Lutz leaned back in the armchair, relaxed and satisfied. 'Tell me who you had in mind to offer my clients.'

'I'd like to do it the other way around. May I?'

'By all means.'

'You have an Englishman named Summers. Captain John Summers. He is in a special section in one of the Gulag camps.' Shapiro looked at a card he took from his jacket pocket. 'Gulag number 704913.' Shapiro watched Lutz's face carefully as he said, 'We had in mind suggesting an exchange with a man who calls himself Gordon Arnold Lonsdale. We believe that he is a Soviet citizen. It seems that his wife might be named Galyusha and that she lives in Moscow with their two children.'

181

Lutz put on his glasses and looked at his list again. After a few moments he said, 'He is in Wormwood Scrubs prison, yes?' He looked up at Shapiro. 'Sentenced to twenty-five years' imprisonment.'

'That's the one.'

'He has two associates. They call themselves Kroger or Cohen. Would they be included?'

'I'm quite sure that they could be part of a deal.'

Lutz shifted in the chair and looked towards the window then back at Shapiro.

'This is the first of these exchanges that you've been involved with, Mr Shapiro, is it not? At least, the first when you did the negotiating.'

'Yes.'

'But they briefed you on how we go about it?'

'What particular aspect were you thinking of?'

'Long long ago, nineteen forty-seven or thereabouts, we did the first deal. We took nearly a year and by the time the year was up your man – an American – had died. And Moscow's man – a Czech – had escaped.' He sighed. 'Both sides agreed that if exchanges were to be made in the future we didn't haggle like Armenian carpet-dealers. We said, right from the start, what we wanted and what we would offer in return. If that was not possible then one further offer. If that was not acceptable we shook hands and it was over. We never discuss those people again. Ever. It became an unwritten, unofficial rule of the game. We could tell our superiors or not, as we chose. They would learn one way or another that we were not hagglers, not stooges. But intermediaries. You understand?'

'I think so.'

'So we stop playing games with one another . . .' He paused, '. . . and I set a good example, yes?'

Shapiro half-smiled. 'Please do.'

'OK. The man my friends in Moscow would like to exchange for your man calls himself Reino Hayhanen. His real name is something else. He is half-Finnish,

182

half-Russian and at the moment he is protected by the CIA.'

Shapiro sat down facing Lutz. 'OK. No bargaining, Herr Lutz. The CIA will not exchange Hayhanen for anybody. That is absolutely certain.' Shapiro paused for a moment. 'Is there anyone else that your friends have in mind?'

'Make me an offer, Mr Shapiro. Show me that you understand what we are here for. Tell me who you put on offer for your man.'

'Colonel Rudolph Abel. He is serving a thirty-year sentence in jail in Atlanta, Georgia.'

For a few moments Lutz was silent, then he said, 'Quite frankly, you surprise me.'

'Why?'

'I seem to remember reading that the parents of the young pilot had been in contact with the Soviet Embassy in Washington to suggest an exchange. Their son for Colonel Abel.'

'I don't think the American government feel that that is a fair exchange.'

'But why should they prefer an Englishman instead of an American?'

'We have asked for their collaboration and they have agreed.'

Lutz smiled and stood up. 'You must be very tired after your journey or I'd suggest that I go to my office a couple of blocks away and talk with my clients. And then come back and talk with you.'

'I'd be very happy to do that. I'd like to get it settled, one way or another.'

Lutz stopped with his hand on the doorknob. 'That's something we didn't discuss Mr Shapiro. What if my clients can't find their way to co-operate?'

Shapiro shrugged. 'That would be the end of the matter so far as we were concerned.'

'You wouldn't be prepared to go ahead with the rumoured exchange of Abel for the American pilot?'

'No.'

'May I ask why not?' Lutz said softy.

'As I said earlier. It's a grossly uneven exchange – a senior KGB officer for a young plane pilot. It's not on, Mr Lutz. I'm sure your clients will realise that.'

It was almost midnight when Lutz returned. He wasted no time As he sat down he said, 'My people's reaction was not entirely what I hoped for.' As he saw the grim look on Shapiro's face he shook his head. 'No great problem, Mr Shapiro. In fact, general agreement but with two sets of conditions. Conditions that I think you will find acceptable.'

'What are the conditions?'

'Let me give you the situation as it now is. The case of your man Kretski – Summers – there is no problem. He can be exchanged.' Lutz shrugged. 'The problem of course was Hayhanen. The hard-liners in the KGB would obviously like to get their hands on such a man. A man who betrayed his trust in every possible way.

'Then we come to Powers, the pilot. He is no longer of any interest to Moscow. He was tried and sentenced publicly. He confessed. He served his purpose. He can be released too. That would allow the exchange to be made public.

'So we come to Colonel Abel. An honourable man who has behaved as we should expect a Soviet citizen to behave who fell foul of – shall we say – antagonistic authority.'

Lutz leaned back in the chair. 'So, reluctantly, the exchange you ask for will be accepted. Provided . . .' and Lutz wagged a monitory finger, '. . . provided we can agree on the two sets of conditions. Condition number one I imagine is no real problem. It is what you want as much as my friends do. I refer to complete secrecy. Not just at the time of the exchange, but permanently. No hints in the press. No books, no articles about a spy who came in from the cold. You know what I mean?'

'Of course. Both sides have a vested interest in keeping it secret.'

'And complete denial if there should ever be questions from the media or in Parliament or Congress?'

'Definitely. No problem. What's the second condition?'

'The second condition is just an act to show good faith.' He paused. 'If at some time in the future we should want an exchange for Gordon Lonsdale and the Krogers it would be seriously considered.'

'You know the problem that arises from that?'

'I can think of one – but you tell me.'

'My people could perhaps visualise some innocent British subject being arrested in Moscow and accused of espionage just to effect an exchange for Lonsdale and the Krogers.'

Lutz shrugged. 'I can only assure you, my friend, that that is not likely to happen. My people are not all that concerned about Lonsdale's fate – or the Krogers' for that matter.'

'OK.' Shapiro nodded. 'I agree to both conditions.' He paused. 'How can we arrange the details of the exchanges? Dates, locations, et cetera.'

'How long are you prepared to stay on in Berlin, Mr Shapiro?'

'If it pushes things along I'll stay however long it takes.'

32

Soon after the midnight head count at the Atlanta prison two men showed the release note to the Warden. Half an hour later prisoner number 80016–A was roused from his sleep and told to dress. Rudolph Abel dressed slowly and meticulously and then walked with the two FBI agents to the waiting car.

The Delta jet took off promptly at 2 a.m. and at 5.30 a.m. Abel was taken into the federal detention house on West Street, New York. Throughout the next day, Wednesday, the prisoner was kept out of the way of anyone who could possibly recognise him, apart from the agents guarding him.

Twice, a time was set for his departure, and twice it was cancelled, but on the Thursday afternoon the clearance came through. The car holding Abel was the middle car in a three-car convoy heading for McGuire Air Force Base. When they drove into the base Abel and the two agents transferred into a station wagon which drove down the runway right up to the waiting plane.

It was a big Super-Constellation transport plane usually at the disposal of a USAAF general. Spacious and comfortable, its curtains drawn. The crew waited confined in the cockpit until 6 p.m., when they were given orders to take off. Neither the captain nor the navigator had any idea where they were heading for. But once they were air-borne they were told that they were on a secret mission and their destination was Wiesbaden. But they were not told who they were carrying on board or any details apart from their destination.

Just the fact that Moscow had agreed to Abel's return made the controllers of the operation especially cautious. With the cynicism of their trade they had considered the possibility that Moscow's previous indifference to having Abel back could be because he was out of favour. The possibility that Abel's restlessness could be because he was, in fact, apprehensive as to his fate now he was on his way back made them search him again thoroughly to make sure that he had no means in his clothes or on his body of committing suicide.

It was six o'clock the next morning when the plane landed at Wiesbaden. There was a technicians' meeting because of a fault in the aircraft's radio system that required servicing. The curtains around the passenger seats were drawn so that the repairman could not see Abel and his guards.

The repairman reported that the radio wasn't serviceable, it would have to be replaced. Just over two hours later the plane was edging into the control pattern of the Berlin Air Corridor. For the last half-hour of the two-and-a-half-hour flight to Berlin the plane was under surveillance by three squadrons of MiG fighters. It was 3 p.m. when the plane landed at Tempelhof. The US Provost Marshal was there and one of the military police cars drove Abel and his escort to the US Army Base.

Abel spent the night in a small, grim cell clad only in pyjamas, watched over continuously by a double guard who were changed every two hours. His escorts slept as badly as Abel did but in the comparative comfort of a private house.

At 7.30 the next morning, Saturday February 10, Abel was driven to the Glienicke bridge. The car and its escorting vehicles pulled up at the entrance to Schloss Glienicke and there were officials already there, including two men busy with walkie-talkies. Then, on a signal from one of the men with radios, the two CIA men walked with Abel to the bridge itself. At the bridge they stopped and Abel was handed a document signed by Robert Kennedy as

187

US Attorney-General and John F. Kennedy as President. The document commuted Colonel Abel's sentence and granted him an official pardon on condition that he never re-entered the United States.

The Glienicke Bridge, with its sandstone piers and approaches, spans two small lakes, and is used solely as a crossing-point for the occupation forces. At the other side of the bridge Gary Powers stood with his KGB guard. Abel was asked to take off his glasses so that the other side could confirm his identity. When both sides had signalled their satisfaction that the man displayed by the other side was their man, Abel was told that he was free to cross the bridge.

Picking up his two cases he walked forward, passed Gary Powers just before the demarcation line. Neither acknowledged the other and the transaction was over.

In Washington the lawns of the White House were sprinkled with snow. In the Blue Room Lester Lanin and his orchestra were playing for the guests at a going-away party for the President's brother-in-law and sister. At two o'clock several top government officials discreetly left the room and an hour later Pierre Salinger, the President's press secretary, announced the repatriation of Abel to the Soviet Union and Gary Powers' release to the US authorities. Neither at the party nor in the press room was any great interest aroused by the event.

Joe Shapiro climbed awkwardly into the front passenger seat of the ambulance and told the driver to start. The streets of Brunswick were already crowded with people going to work and traffic, and it was almost an hour before they were approaching the border-crossing at Helmstedt. Trails of mist swirled across from the woods on each side of the road.

Already there was a long queue of cars. Not at the usual crossing-point barriers but nearly a quarter of a mile from the frontier post. At the temporary pole barrier Shapiro showed his ID card and the operational order to the Field

Security sergeant. The sergeant checked them carefully and then waved to the military policeman who raised the counter-weighted pole.

At the normal control point the ambulance stopped again and Shapiro climbed down. He could see the grey Soviet Army field ambulance at the pole on the far side. From the back of the British ambulance two men got down. One was an SIS doctor and the other was Hugh Morton.

The three men walked to the white painted control post and Shapiro lifted the phone, speaking slowly and distinctly in Russian. He listened for a moment and then hung up. He nodded to the other two and the barriers of both sides of the crossing control lifted slowly.

The two ambulances rolled forward and stopped. The rear doors of both vehicles were opened and latched and two Soviets in civilian clothes eased a stretcher down the sloping metal runners. A KGB man in major's uniform waved Shapiro over. Shapiro looked at the face of the man on the stretcher then back at the KGB man. They exchanged a few words, the officer nodded and Shapiro signalled to the doctor to come over. They rolled the stretcher to the British ambulance and waited for the ramp to lift it into the back of the ambulance. When it had been latched in place, Shapiro spoke to the driver then got in the back of the ambulance, followed by the doctor and Morton. As the rear doors were closed Shapiro looked at the doctor.

'Well?'

'He looks in a pretty bad way but I'd need to examine him before I pass any comment.' He paused. 'Will you pass me that clamp?'

The doctor adjusted the drip and then Shapiro banged on the back of the driver's cab and the ambulance turned slowly and headed back up the road to Brunswick.

Shapiro looked across at the doctor. 'Is what you've got at the house enough? Or should he go to hospital?'

The doctor shrugged. 'Joe. If what I've got at the house isn't enough there's nothing else at the hospital that can do better. Not at this stage, anyway.'

The big house was in five acres of its own grounds and a room on the ground floor was equipped with all the paraphernalia of a mobile operating theatre and pharmacy.

The doctor and his assistant, masked and sterile, cut the sweat-sodden clothing from the man's shrunken body. No attempt had been made by the Russians to alleviate or hide his condition. Not even a wash or a bandage to give a better impression.

Slowly and gently the doctor checked over the body and the head of the man who lay there with his eyes closed, barely breathing, his teeth clenched tight as if he were resisting pain. Twenty minutes later the doctor gave his instructions to his two assistants and left them to their work.

In the small ante-room he joined Shapiro and Morton. He pulled up a chair and sat down looking at them both.

'In lay terms he's suffering from exhaustion, starvation and various wounds. He may have broken bones or internal injuries but until he's in a suitable condition for a proper examination I can't be certain.'

'What's it add up to, James?' Shapiro's face was grim.

'Now I've looked him over, I'm more hopeful. With a transfusion, a clean-up and a controlled feeding regime a week will make a big difference so far as his body is concerned.'

'What's that mean?'

'It means that I've no way of diagnosing what his mental state might be.' He paused. 'It doesn't look good. He's in coma and shows little or no response to the preliminary neural tests – I'm afraid you'll have to be patient and I'll keep you in touch with his condition.'

Shapiro looked at Morton. 'I'll stay here with him, Hughie. You get back to London. They need you and there's nothing you can do here that I can't do.'

The doctor interrupted. 'If you'll excuse me I'll get on with my job.'

When the doctor had left Morton said, 'What do you think? Will he make it?'

Shapiro sighed heavily. 'If you mean will he live – yes. I'd put my last dollar on it. But if you mean more than that – ' Shapiro shook his head. 'I don't know. He looks bad to me. He's going to need a lot of psychiatric help. You'd better warn them back in London.'

Morton stood up. 'Get some rest, Joe. Get some sleep. Don't dwell on it. Give it time. You've got to be patient.'

By the end of a week Shapiro was really worried and had asked for a second opinion and Morton sent over a neuro-surgeon who checked over the doctor's notes and examined the patient. When he saw Shapiro afterwards he confirmed that the physical diagnosis was correct.

'Physically he's recovered remarkably well. The broken ribs and the bones in his hands we can deal with in a few weeks' time. But the central nervous system has taken a lot of punishment.' He paused. 'As you know he's no longer in coma. But his hearing is negligible and although there seems to be no damage to the vocal chords he doesn't speak. He can see all right but at the moment he is literally both deaf and dumb. And I suspect that that is psychological – trauma. That's going to take quite a time to treat. And it may or may not be curable. I just don't know.'

'How long will it take to find out?'

'Months rather than weeks.'

'And to cure?'

The surgeon shrugged. 'I've no idea. It could take years. But on the other hand he could recover overnight. Not from anything we can do. Just mother nature doing her stuff. Spontaneous healing.'

'And that's all you can say?'

'I'm afraid so. But if it's any consolation I should think that he will be fit enough to get up and walk around –

191

with help – in a matter of days. He's got an amazing constitution, that chap.'

Five days later there was a vast physical improvement. The man called Phoenix had put on weight and his ribs and hands had been strapped and the X-rays showed that the bones were knitting together satisfactorily. He walked slowly and uncertainly but without a stick or any other aid. The washed-out pale blue eyes stared rather than looked, and his mouth was always shut tight, the teeth clenched and the muscles taut at the sides of his mouth. But there was no visible response to the words or sounds. Sometimes Joe Shapiro reached out and gripped the man's heavy forearm as they sat in the spring sunshine in the garden. The flesh was firm and warm but there was never any reaction.

Part Three

33

The man named Johnny had paid for a meal for them both and Josef felt uncomfortable in the hotel restaurant in his cheap, drab clothing, but Johnny didn't seem to notice. They were drinking their coffee when Johnny said, 'Did you see in the paper that Lenin died yesterday?'

Josef nodded. 'Yes, I saw it.'

'What difference will it make?'

The young man shrugged. 'The fight will be out in the open now.'

'Between who?'

'Stalin, Trotsky, Zinoviev and maybe Rykov.'

'And who will come out on top?'

Josef laughed. 'Lenin?'

'I don't understand. Lenin's dead.'

'Trotsky is finished, Stalin will cash in on Lenin's reputation, Lenin will become a kind of Bolshevik saint, and the others will go along with Stalin.'

'I heard rumours that Lenin had recommended that Stalin had become too powerful and should be removed from the Central Committee.'

The young man looked at him for long moments before he replied. 'You're not a journalist are you?'

'What makes you say that?'

'Only people right inside the Party know anything about rumours like that.'

'There are a lot of rumours going around about the Bolsheviks. Lenin was poisoned was one I heard. There were plenty of others too.'

'Yeah. But yours wasn't a rumour. It was the real

thing. And you know it was. A journalist isn't going to get information like that.'

Johnny smiled. 'You've got a sharp mind Josef. They must have taught you well in Moscow.'

'Maybe.'

'What are you going to do now you're back?'

'Anything that will keep me alive and let me spend my free time making them pay for what they have done to me and my family.'

'How are you going to do that?'

Josef shrugged helplessly. 'I've no idea. But I'll find some way.'

'It won't be easy, Josef. There are a lot of people in this country who believe in Communism. Not just workers but influential people.'

Josef half-smiled. 'You don't understand do you?'

'Understand what?'

'I'm not against Communism. Communism would work. What they've got in Moscow isn't Communism. It's Bolshevism. And that's a very different thing.'

'Was it what they did to your family that disillusioned you?'

'No. I was disillusioned before. I was on the inside. I knew what they were doing. At first I thought it was just a temporary thing that would be over in a few months. But it wasn't. It was obscene. The Party philosophers writing pamphlets and theses about a brave new world and behind them groups of men fighting like savages for power.' He shook his head sadly. 'Nobody could believe or understand what went on unless they were on the inside and saw it happening.'

'Where are you going to live?'

'I'll probably stay here if I can find work. It doesn't matter to me where I live.'

'Would you consider moving to London if there was work for you there?'

'I'd move to Land's End. It makes no odds to me where I live.'

196

'I know people who could give you work.'

'Doing what?'

'Translating.'

'Translating what?'

'Newspapers, documents – that sort of thing. From Russian into English.'

'How much would I get?'

'Five pounds a week.'

Josef shook his head, smiling. 'I'm twenty-two and nobody's gonna pay somebody that age five quid a week.'

'Why don't you put it to the test?'

'What sort of firm is this we're talking about?'

'It's a small government department but you'd work at home.'

'Do you work for this place?'

'I work for the department that is setting up this new service.'

'You know that I've got no education, no qualifications.'

'You may have no formal qualifications but you've got all the qualifications we're looking for.' The man leaned forward and put his hand gently on Josef's leg. 'We'll look after you.'

And those words to the orphanage boy meant more than the man who called himself Johnny could have known. After a lifetime of looking after himself the words were like balm to his raw, wounded mind. They travelled together to London the following day.

34

Johnny had found him a small flat in one of the rows of
Victorian houses on the south side of the river at Putney.
It turned out that Johnny was Major Johnson. But he
could tell that he wasn't a normal soldier. He never wore
uniform and seemed to be able to come and go as he
pleased. But he was obviously a man with considerable
authority. He made instant personal decisions when it was
necessary. To his surprise his wages were paid promptly,
and in cash, every Friday afternoon.

Johnny had bought him dictionaries and a supply of
paper for the typewriter, and the material he had to
translate was varied. Sometimes an article from *Pravda*,
sometimes the minutes of a Party committee meeting in
Moscow or Leningrad. There were frequent reports of
the organisation of secret Party cells in other European
countries, and confidential reports on industry and agriculture in various parts of the Soviet Union. He was not
allowed to keep copies and sometimes a woman's voice
on the telephone would raise queries about some point
of English in his translation. He apologised for his poor
English but she never commented back.

They had asked him to change his name to Smith and
had given him a back-dated insurance card in that name.
And his wages came in a plain brown envelope marked
'S' and he was asked to sign for them just with the letter
'S'. He had been given no special working hours nor was
pressure put on him to get work done in a hurry, but
he worked a full nine-hour day every day of the week
including weekends.

It was almost nine months after he had started work for Johnny Johnson that he was asked if he would deliver a small package to a man in Paris. The address was in the rue Mouffetard, two rooms over a *pâtisserie* and a man who looked as if he was dying, his face was so gaunt and pale. He was invited inside and he went in reluctantly. But inside, although it was incredibly untidy, it was like so many of those small rooms that he had delivered messages to in Moscow. Even an icon set in a space on the crowded bookshelves and an etching of Karl Marx in a wooden frame on the wall.

The old man pointed to a box with a blanket folded on top of it and when Josef sat down he was handed a small glass of vodka. The old man sat on the ramshackle bed and looked at his messenger.

'What's your name, young man?'

'I don't give my name to strangers, mister.'

'And quite right too.' He paused. 'When are you going back to London?'

'That's my business.'

The old man cackled. 'You sound like one of those bastards from the Cheka.' He paused. 'You ever heard of the Cheka?'

'Yes. I've heard of it.'

'I got something for you to take back with you to London.' He paused. 'You want it now?'

'Is it small?'

'Yeah. But I'll have to wrap it up for you.' The old man stood up and walked awkwardly to the book-shelves and took down a thin yellow book. As he walked back Josef noticed the old man's strenuous efforts to walk and for the first time noticed his mis-shapen leg. When the man stumbled he jumped up to save him from falling. As his arms went round the man's frail body he saw the man's teeth as he fought against the pain.

'Are you OK, Mr Lukas? Shall I get you some help? A doctor maybe.'

199

Lukas shook his head. 'No. It will go. Just let me sit down.' When he was seated Lukas looked at Josef and said, 'When people talk about the brave new world in Moscow just think of my leg, my friend. A present from the comrades.'

'What happened?'

'I had a small printing business. A man asked me to print something for him. I never read it. I was too busy. It was a resolution to the Politburo by Trotsky. They beat me up in the old insurance office in Dzerzhinski Square that the Ve-Cheka have taken over. The doctors say I'll have to put up with it or have my leg taken off.'

'Are you a White Russian?'

For the first time Josef saw Lukas laugh. 'Me? I'm not White nor Red nor any other bloody colour. I'm just a Russian who hates those bastards who broke up my body.'

Josef glanced at the paper cover of the yellow book that Lukas had handed to him. The legend on the cover, in Russian, described the contents as a résumé of the Twelfth Congress of the CPSU. He looked up at Lukas and said, 'You'd better cover it up. Have you got some paper we can wrap it in?'

Lukas smiled and said quietly, 'So you can read Russian, my friend?'

Josef shrugged. 'Perhaps. What about the wrapping paper?'

Ten minutes later, with the document wrapped, Josef stood at the door and turned to look at the old man. He said in Russian, 'You're working against them aren't you?' When the old man nodded Josef said, 'I'm sorry about what they did to you. Some day it will change.'

'Goodbye, young man. But stop dreaming dreams. Nothing will change. But we can hurt them by letting the world know what they do to their own working-people.'

Major Johnson had asked him about the hour or so that he spent with Lukas. He listened intently as Josef told him what had been said, but he asked no more questions and

200

had not pursued the matter. But when Josef was leaving Johnson said, 'What did you think of Lukas?'

'He's very lonely. And very sick.'

Johnson nodded but said nothing more.

It was almost four months later when Major Johnson asked him if he would be prepared to go to Paris for a few months to help Lukas, who found it more difficult to get around. Josef had pointed out that he spoke no French but Johnson said it didn't matter. The only people he would be dealing with were Russians. It never entered his mind to refuse and he had left for Paris a week later.

But in that week Johnson had briefed him carefully about his new duties in Paris. His job would be to liaise with groups of Russians who were anti-Bolshevik. In some cases anti-Revolution as well. He was to pass funds and messages to them and tell them what London wanted in return. He was warned that they were not easy to deal with. Not only differing convictions and objectives but forceful, independent leaders who quarrelled bitterly among themselves. He was to keep an eye on what they were doing, interpret their usefulness to London and try and hold the peace between them.

Before he left for Paris a meeting had been arranged by Major Johnson. It was at the St Ermin's Hotel and the man's name was Mason. Just the two of them. He was about the same age as Johnson but not so easy-going. He had asked Josef about his time in Moscow and Leningrad. He talked slowly as if he was slow in absorbing what was said, digesting it before he asked the next question. But as the chat went on Josef realised that Mason wasn't slow-minded or stupid, he was just a very clever interrogator. Never asking the same question twice as if he doubted the truth of what Josef said, but frequently crossing the tracks of what had been said, checking obliquely but with that innocent country-bumpkin look of trying hard to understand what he was being told. What also seemed odd was that, unlike this man, Major Johnson had never asked him about his time in Russia.

Johnson had seen him off on the boat-train at Victoria and had said that Mason was much impressed by Josef's attitude. Josef had no idea what he meant. He hadn't had an attitude. He'd just answered some questions. He'd been given a hundred pounds for his expenses in Paris, in cash. More money than he had ever handled in his life before.

The old man, Lukas, had helped him find a room for himself in the rue Mouffetard at the back of a butcher's shop. He had paid for Lukas to see a doctor and gone with him to the surgery. The doctor had come out of his small office and told Josef that Lukas was terminally ill. He had no more than a few months to live.

But it was nearly two years later when the old man died and in the meantime Josef had consolidated his relationships with the various groups in contact with Lukas. It was all a vivid reminder of his early days in Moscow. The committees, the resolutions, the speeches and pamphlets and the rivalries. Nevertheless, the contacts those groups had in the Soviet Union were widespread and in all walks of life. Josef talked and listened and painstakingly typed out his reports and delivered them in sealed envelopes to a man at the British Embassy, to be forwarded to London via the diplomatic bag. From time to time London asked him to pursue certain items but there was no pressure of any kind. His wages had been increased to ten pounds a week when he moved to Paris and they paid the rent for his room in Putney while he was away.

Lukas died in the summer of 1927 and there was only Josef and Major Johnson at his funeral. The people in London had paid for everything. After it was over they went back to Josef's room. Johnson said they should have a talk.

He was to be given a new name – Sanders, and he was to have new responsibilities. He would take over Lukas's job and also be responsible for maintaining contact with anti-Bolshevik groups in Berlin.

Two years later he was pulled back to London with the suggestion that he should have formal education in the Russian language. He never saw himself as having a choice in how his life should be. He counted himself lucky to be so well-paid. The Russian course took a year and then he was interviewed by Mason again. This time in a private room at the Reform Club.

'Remind me,' Mason said. 'What do we call you these days?'

'Sanders, sir. Josef Sanders.'

'Yes, of course. You did very well on your Russian course. Your tutor says you speak more fluently than he does.'

'He kept telling me that I'd never learn the grammar of Russian because I didn't know the grammar of my own language.' Josef smiled. 'I never could work out the difference between accusative and dative.'

'Ah, yes.' Mason looked embarrassed at the frankness, or the ignorance. It was hard to tell which. He shifted uneasily in the big leather armchair. 'I'd like to put a suggestion to you if I may.'

'Whatever you want is OK with me, Mr Mason.'

'Kind of you, I'm sure. Let me explain first before you agree. I – we – would like you to be put on a more official, more substantial footing. You have done valuable work for us in your own modest way and there is much else that we would like you to do that could not be done by a civilian.' He paused and shuffled his body again. 'Briefly, I am authorised to offer you a commission as a full lieutenant in the army.' He sat back slapping his thighs with both hands as if he was glad to get done with a rather dubious proposition.

'I don't know anything about soldiering, Mr Mason.'

'Of course not. Of course not. You wouldn't have to

203

do any of that. It's just a device – a way – of making you official, giving you some proper standing in the service.'

'I don't understand, Mr Mason. What service are we talking about?'

'Who do you think you're working for?'

'Major Johnson said it was a small government department that was interested in what is going on in the Soviet Union.'

'And you didn't wonder why a government department should be interested in those things?'

Josef shrugged. 'No. It's not my business.'

'Well. I suppose that's a point of view.' He paused. 'A very practical point of view if I may say so.' Mason leaned forward awkwardly. 'We're a department that is responsible for collecting intelligence about the Soviet Union.'

'You mean research?'

'It's rather more than that, Josef. The government doesn't like what's happening in Russia.'

Josef laughed sharply. 'A lot of Russians don't like it either.'

'Exactly,' Mason said. 'And I understand from the major that you don't like it either. The things they did to your family. Is that so?'

Josef nodded. 'Yes.'

'There are others involved in this but you've got an advantage over them. You know all about it from the inside. You're a very valuable man to us and we want to make you even more valuable.'

'Like I said, Mr Mason. I'll do whatever you want. You don't need to persuade me.'

When Johnson talked to him about his meeting with Mason he had obviously been amused at Josef's description of the encounter. He sat down heavily in the cane chair and looked at Josef.

'You know, my friend, it's time you changed.'

'Changed what?'

204

'Every bloody thing. You're not a cabin-boy on an old tub of a boat now. What old Mason said is right. You're a valuable man.' When he saw the smile on Josef's face he said sharply, 'Grow up, Josef. This isn't just a job, this is a career. Make something of it. Don't be so bloody humble. You said you wanted to fight those bastards who killed your wife and you just go on like a maiden aunt.'

When Josef didn't reply Johnson said, 'I've recommended that you should do three months' basic training in the army before you're commissioned.'

Josef just shrugged.

Johnson's hunch about how to stiffen up his protégé was not arrived at without a lot of thought. He knew too much of Josef's background not to realise that you don't come out of an orphanage to being a cabin-boy on an old tramp steamer with any great confidence in yourself or the world. And what had happened after must have been like a dream turning into a nightmare. But his ploy worked. Josef came out of his three months' training a different man. A new self-confidence, no longer the humble orphanage boy. Johnson had given him a copy of the official warrant for the King's Commission. He was now, despite his civilian clothes, Lieutenant Josef Sanders, General Service.

Lieutenant Sanders tackled his work with the groups with authority when he went back to Paris, and his instructions from London were now more demanding. It was no longer just a matter of listening to the information that came out of the groups' contacts in Russia but passing on demands for specific information. Gradually the groups were turned into cells of actual intelligence gathering. The information that they produced was low-level but it covered a wide spectrum of the political and economic life in the Soviet Union. And it was almost the only intelligence available to London.

His visits to Berlin became more frequent and more important. By 1933 the rise of the Nazi Party had made

Moscow put pressure on the Cheka to try and recruit the Russian counter-revolutionaries in Germany with pardons for past defections. Sanders worked actively against the Cheka recruitment of any of his contacts and was largely successful. Both in Paris and Berlin his guidance was respected and he was seen as a man of authority. And although his new official status was never revealed it was taken for granted that his authority flowed from official sources in London.

When it became obvious that the Berlin groups were more active and purposeful than those in Paris, Josef was moved to Berlin. Johnson had wondered if past events in Berlin would lead to objections from Josef but when he put the suggestion of the move to him it was clear that Josef welcomed the challenge.

By 1938 Josef was a major in the Intelligence Corps and was now spending more time in London. SIS was now trying desperately to reorganise itself to meet the demands of the war with Germany that was obviously coming. He was put in charge of all intelligence aimed at the Soviet Union and his advice was frequently sought on matters concerning the Soviet attempts to penetrate British life.

On the Sunday morning of September 3, 1939, when war was declared on Nazi Germany, Major Sanders's identity was changed once again. He was now, officially, Major Joseph Shapiro, thirty-seven years old, and a long-serving and senior officer of MI6.

35

When Hitler gave the order to launch Operation Barbarossa on June 22, 1941 the Soviet Union and Great Britain became allies. Uncomfortable allies.

In the next six months the Nazi hordes took city after city. Brest-Litovsk, Kiev, Kharkov, Rostov and Smolensk. And in mid-October the Soviet Government left Moscow in what looked like the last few days before the Nazis took the city. In North Africa Rommel had taken over the Afrika Korps. Joseph Kennedy, the United States Ambassador to Britain, counselled his government to abandon the British to their fate.

Then in December 1941 two things happened. It was obvious that the Germans were not able to take Moscow against its grim defence. And at the end of the first week the Japanese attacked Pearl Harbor and the United States was reluctantly in the war.

It was in December that the British allowed the Soviet Union to set up a liaison unit in London. Members of the Red Army gave speeches to workers in munitions factories, negotiators pleaded for more and more supplies of medicines, medical equipment and arms, and propagandists urged an Allied invasion of France. Inevitably there were members of the Soviet liaison unit whose objectives were subversive.

A separate entity was the Soviet Military Mission. And it was the mission that came under the closest scrutiny of the British intelligence services. The mission consisted of representatives of the Soviet Army, Navy and Airforce and they were responsible for exchanging information about their mutual Axis enemies. Orders of Battle, captured documents and military intelligence. The exchanges were so cautious and the two sides so suspicious of each other that little of real help came from the meetings for either side. The fact that the Soviets were willing to maintain the mission in London despite its ineffectiveness was the basis for the British suspicion that some members of the mission had more covert functions. There were seven members of the mission who were suspected of being NKVD officers. The files on the suspects were passed to Joe Shapiro.

Each file had photographs of the suspect and brief details of his movements and contacts during his time in London. It was the file marked Abromov, Nikolai, that had Shapiro's attention. Not the report itself which had nothing of any real significance. Contacts with journalists, minor politicians and visits to art galleries. It was the photographs that made him stop. Photographs of Abromov with various people. Some identified, some not. But it was the Russian's face that stayed in his mind. He had seen him somewhere before. His mind went back over his counter-revolutionary groups in Berlin. There was a connection with Berlin. He was almost certain that it was Berlin.

Shapiro decided that he should find some excuse for meeting the man casually, with other people rather than alone, so that his intent was not obvious. It was a week before there was a suitable occasion. An informal get-together so that the mission could meet some of the Eighth Army officers who had started the defeat of Rommel in the desert. The reception was in one of the conference rooms at the War Office, and Shapiro had gone with Johnson and two of Johnson's colleagues from his old regiment.

The high-ceilinged, panelled room with ornate chandeliers was crowded when they arrived, with much laughter and the usual rounds of toasts already livening

208

things up as the various victories of the two allies were being celebrated in vodka and whisky, one by one. After fifteen minutes slowly circulating among the groups of people Shapiro had not seen the man named Nikolai Abromov. He was thinking of leaving when he saw him. They saw each other in the same moment and neither of them could believe what he saw. Shapiro was in battledress with Intelligence Corps' green-based major's crowns on his shoulder straps and the man going under the name of Abromov was wearing his duty green uniform, jacket, breeches and black boots with a full colonel's three stars on his shoulder bands. But they had both seen the recognition in the other's eyes.

Shapiro nodded towards the door and the Russian acknowledged the indication. In the empty corridor they stood facing one another.

Shapiro took the proffered hand. 'Nice to see you, Zag.'

Zagorsky smiled. 'Nice to see you too, young Josef.' He paused. 'Can we talk?'

'Of course. Let's go to my place. It's not too far away.'

As Shapiro brewed them some tea Zagorsky looked around the room. The white walls bare of any kind of relief or decoration except for three shelves of books. Books in Russian, French, German and English but almost every one covering the history of Russia, from the days of the Tsars to the first year of the war.

When they were sitting in the only two chairs in the room Shapiro said quietly, 'Who talks first?'

Zagorsky smiled. 'It might as well be me. Or you'll think I've risen from the dead.'

Shapiro said softly, 'And I believe you could if you wanted to enough. When I saw you being almost carried out of that court-room I thought it was all over for you. What the hell happened?'

Zagorsky said, 'Your Russian is really excellent, how did you get that good?'

'They sent me to university. Anyway, tell me what happened.'

'What did you think had happened?'

'I only heard rumours. Rumours that you had been shot the same day, rumours that you were in Siberia in a labour-camp. The usual rumours one hears in these cases.'

'They *were* going to shoot me. The next day. And then, late that night Dzerzhinski sent for me. He saw me himself. He had the transcript of my trial in front of him, including my rather emotional outburst in court.

'He said that he had been impressed by my work at Ve-Cheka and because he himself was originally a Pole he was aware of the harassment of Poles by certain Soviets. He said too that the military judge had been angered by being dragged into what was essentially political harassment and had spoken to him angrily.

'He said that he could offer me a way out. If I agreed to going underground as a Cheka officer my sentence would be struck out. The record would be wiped clean.'

'Did you accept?'

Zagorsky smiled. 'Of course I did. I told him to let the trial and the verdict stand. It would provide me with perfect cover. Like you, everybody would assume that I was dead.' He laughed. 'You couldn't have better cover than that.'

'Can I ask you what you've been doing since then?'

'You can ask, but that uniform you're wearing means that the answers will be cautious.'

'Tell me what you can.'

'I went down to Samarkand and ran a network of illegals into Iran and Afghanistan. Then like you I went to university to improve my foreign languages. Mainly my English.' He smiled. 'And now I'm here.'

'Spying on us.'

'Collecting information let us say. And what about you? How is the family?'

For long moments Shapiro looked at Zagorsky and then said softly, 'Are you kidding?'

The Russian looked genuinely surprised. 'I don't understand.'

'You mean you never asked what had happened to us?'

'I went straight down to Samarkand the next day. I was there for two years. A lot had changed by the time I got back to Moscow. A lot of people were no longer there. One didn't ask what had happened to them or where they'd gone.'

'What was the last you heard of me?'

'As I remember it you were in Warsaw with your wife and child. A son wasn't it?'

'Yes. It was a son. When you were put on trial we were in court. They forced us to go. My wife, Anna, was Polish and she was very upset. Not only about you but what the Polish Bolsheviks were planning to do in Poland. We escaped to Berlin. I got a job in a bar. Washing-up at first and later on as a barman.

'I came back one night and found that my wife had been murdered. Garotted. And they stamped a red star on her wrist. They took my small son away. I don't know what happened to him.'

For several minutes Zagorsky just sat there and Shapiro could see that he was genuinely shocked. Then the Russian took a deep breath.

'Saying I'm sorry won't help, Josef. Nevertheless I am sorry. I can't bear to think about it happening. It sickens me.'

'All for the good of the Party, comrade?'

Zagorsky shook his head. 'I won't attempt to make excuses. There are no excuses that would satisfy me. And there are none that would satisfy you.' He paused and sighed. 'And that's why you're wearing that uniform.'

'I never needed a uniform, Zag. It's my life's work to fight you people.'

'We're not all murderers, Josef. You know better than that.'

'You're all part of it. You know it goes on but you never raise a voice to stop it. You may not be a murderer, Zag.

211

But you're an accessory to murder. And in my book the one is as evil as the other.'

'Do you include yourself in that? You must have known a lot of what was going on when you and Anna were working for me.'

'I don't excuse myself but I take comfort from the fact that I was very young, I thought it would change and when it didn't I escaped.' He paused. 'I'd rather be a coward than a murderer, Zag.'

'When did this happen in Berlin?'

'About twenty years ago.'

'And you've hated Russians for nearly twenty years.'

'No. I loved the Russians. I just hate Bolsheviks.'

'Including me?'

'No. You didn't have any part in murdering my wife. They were ready to murder you if it had suited them. I'm just sorry for you.'

'Is there any way – short of treason – that I can try and make up for that terrible thing?'

'Yeah, come over to us and work against them.'

'I said short of treason.'

'Are you married Zag?'

'No. I don't live the kind of life that goes with marriage.'

'How long are you staying in London with the mission?'

'I was posted here permanently. But I shall put in for a transfer now.'

'Why?'

'It would be pointless for me to stay. You know too much about me and I wouldn't relish working against you.'

'Can I ask you something personal?'

'Of course.'

'Did you ever really believe in the Bolsheviks? Especially way back when we were on that boat?'

Zagorsky closed his eyes, his face turned up towards the ceiling as he thought. Then he opened his eyes and looked at Shapiro.

'It's a tough question to answer, Josef. I need to search my heart. On the boat I think the answer has to be "yes".

I believed in Communism, especially Lenin's version of it. Not Trotsky's and not Stalin's – although he wasn't all that important in those days. So Communism I believed in, but Bolshevism I wasn't sure about. Let's say I gave it the benefit of the doubt. There were harsh things to be done to organise the country. At least the Bolsheviks were determined enough and ruthless enough to do what was necessary.'

'How long did you go on believing in them?'

'Until my trial. I knew then that one didn't have to be guilty of anything beyond the greed and envy of rivals to lose one's freedom or one's life. After the deal was done with Dzerzhinski I just switched off my mind so far as politics were concerned. I made my work, my life.' He shrugged. 'Maybe not my life – more an existence.' He sighed. 'Not a hero's story, my friend. But the truth.'

It was too near the pattern of Shapiro's own life for him not to recognise its truth. He looked at Zagorsky's gaunt face and was sorry for him.

'Are you going to tell them of our meeting?

'Of our meeting, yes. Your name, no. What we have talked about, no. You were a friendly officer who invited me home for a drink, and following our orders to make contacts with any friendly Englishman, I went to your home. I don't know where it was. You talked on and on about Montgomery and I talked on and on about Timoshenko.'

'So how do you get them to withdraw you?'

'That's no problem. I volunteer for more active duties. The mission is a privileged posting with a long, long waiting list. And the war won't last much longer. Two years perhaps and then we'll all have to pay the bill.'

'What bill is that?'

'The cost of the sacrifices, the price of victory. The Soviet Union having flexed its muscles and found that they work will be ready to advance on the world.'

'Which part of the world?'

Zagorsky stood up slowly, 'Where can I get a taxi?'

213

'On the corner.' He paused. 'You didn't answer my question.'

Zagorsky picked up his white gloves and his cap and as he stood at the door he said quietly, 'You know the answer, Josef, as well as I do. Not a part of the world. Just the world.'

36

When the war in Europe ended Shapiro was posted to 21 Army Group at its HQ in Bad Oynhausen. It was only a few months since the Soviet Union and Britain had been genuine allies, but by the end of 1945 the Red Army was deploying overwhelming forces of infantry and armoured divisions on their side of the Occupation Zone border.

Shapiro's first task was to set up line-crossing operations into the Russian Zone of occupied Germany. Each line-crossing unit was run by a British intelligence officer but the line-crossers were Germans or German-speaking displaced persons. Where possible the crossers were sent to areas that they already knew well. The local hatred of the Red Army's ruthless occupation made it easy to recruit local informants who could supply information on almost any aspect of the occupying forces.

It was in the summer of 1947 when Shapiro got a telephone call from the CO of 70 Field Security Unit in Hildesheim. Line-crossers worked both sides of the zone borders but the Russians had more difficulty in recruiting volunteers from a hostile population. From time to time Field Security Units picked up a line-crosser working for the Russians in the British Zone. A Russian line-crosser had been caught by a detachment of 70 FSU in Göttingen.

'Why are you calling me, Captain?'

'This chap we picked up refuses to talk except to you.'

'To me? Did he know my name?'

'Yes. He gave your name, your rank and he knew that you were at 21 AG headquarters in Bad Oynhausen.'

'Did he say why he wanted to talk to me?'

'No, sir.'
'What's his name?'
'I don't know. He won't talk.'
'How do you know he's working for the other side?'
'He was with a fellow who admitted under interrogation that he was a line-crosser. They both had the same type of forged papers.'
'What's he like?'
'Mid-twenties, well-built, educated. We think he speaks English as well as German.'
'OK. I'll come down in a couple of days. Where are you holding him?'
'In the local prison in Hildesheim.'
'OK. I'll see you on Wednesday.'

It was a pleasant drive down to Hildesheim in the confiscated Mercedes. The old town itself was still largely rubble. For some strange reason or blunder the quiet medieval town had been almost completely wiped out by the US Air Force in the last few weeks of the war. Centuries-old buildings had been reduced to rubble and dust in less than an hour.

70 Field Security's HQ was in a large house on the edge of the town and when Shapiro had been shown around he was offered a room where he could talk to the prisoner from the jail.

An hour later a young man was shown into the room by a sergeant who took off the handcuffs and left. Shapiro sat on the edge of the camp bed looking at the young man.

'What's your name, young man?' he said in German.

'My field name is Lemke,' the young man said and to Shapiro's surprise he spoke in Russian.

'Why do you want to speak to me?'

'I was told to speak to you.'

'By whom?'

'A man whose real name is Zagorsky. He uses other names but he told me to tell you his real name.'

There was a long pause before Shapiro spoke.

'Do you work for him?'

'No. He contacted me about a month ago. He gave me orders to cross the border in this area and to ask to speak to you.'

'You'd better tell me what it's all about.'

'He told me to tell you that it was payment of a debt.'

'A debt. What debt?'

'I don't know. He said to tell you about my family and you would understand.'

Shapiro pointed at a chair. 'Sit down.' When the young man was sitting down Shapiro said, 'OK. Tell me about your family.'

'I never knew about my family. All I can tell you is what Zagorsky told me.'

'Go on.'

'My mother was Polish, my father was English. They married in Moscow but went to work for the Party in Warsaw. Something happened and they fled to Berlin. My mother died a short time after and I was taken away by strangers. I was only two or three years old. I was put in an orphanage near Leningrad.' The young man shrugged. 'That's what he told me to tell you.'

Shapiro sat looking at his son, but all he could think of was Anna. He wished that he could tell her that the boy was safe. Tell her that his hair was as black as hers, his eyes as blue as his father's and his fingers long and slender. And she would say that the boy's firm mouth and strong jaw were all his. It had been twenty-four years since the small boy had been taken away and in his mind's eye he had never changed. Despite the lapse of time he had always thought of his son as a small child in a woollen jersey and leggings and a red knitted hat with a white bobble on top of it. He had no doubt that the young man sitting there was his son. He felt relief to know that he was alive and well but he felt no sudden surge of love and affection. There were things that had to be done. And he would do them, but time and life had ground away his capacity to feel an upsurge of emotion.

217

He should be calling for champagne, telling the world that his long-lost son was found, flinging his arms about those strong young shoulders. But he couldn't bring himself to do it. Maybe in time he could feel that way and do those things. But right now, despite the heavy thumping of his heart, he felt no such emotion.

'Did Zagorsky say anything more to you?'

'He just gave me the instructions on how to come over the Zone border and told me about my family.' The young man smiled diffidently. 'He said that you were a man to be trusted.'

Shapiro stood up. 'Where are your belongings?'

'I only had the papers and a little money. I expected to be caught quite quickly.'

'You say your mother was Polish, do you speak Polish?'

'It's not bad.' He smiled. 'Poles tell me it's very old-fashioned. Out of date slang. But the orphans were mainly Poles.'

Shapiro stood looking at his son. 'I'll take you back with me to my house, and I'll get proper documentation for you.'

'Did this message from Zagorsky make any sense to you?'

'Yes it did. Apart from anything else it means you're under my protection now but you're not under arrest.'

Shapiro had spoken to the Field Security captain and the arrest sheet had been torn up and Shapiro had signed for the take-over of the prisoner. Shapiro had asked for the receipt to be endorsed to establish that the prisoner had not been charged with any offence.

As they got into the car the young man said quietly, 'Can I ask you what this is all about?'

Shapiro started the car as he said, 'I'll tell you later.'

Part Four

37

Sir Peter came in from the garden when he heard Shapiro's car pull into the drive. It didn't really fit the organisation's protocol to be seeing Shapiro without the request coming through Morton and it was even less palatable that Shapiro had made clear that he didn't want Hugh Morton to know about his visit. But Joe Shapiro was MI6's longest-serving officer and Sir Peter was sure that whatever it was all about Shapiro would have good reasons for his request. He glanced in the hall mirror as he walked to the front door. Untidy but clean was his verdict.

The handshakes and greetings were warm and genuine and when they were seated he looked at Shapiro.

'You look tired, Joe. It's time you took some leave.'

'That's what I came to see you about. One of the things anyway.'

'You don't need to see me about that, for heaven's sake. Take what leave you want. When did you last have leave? Must be two years at least. Or is it more?'

'About six years, Sir Peter.' He looked towards the window on the garden and then back at his boss.

'I'm due to retire next June. I wondered if there was any chance of retiring early without my pension being reduced?'

'Of course. No problem at all. Is there some other problem, Joe? You don't look your usual energetic self.'

'Not a problem. But there's something I want to tell you. But I need your assurance that it will stay between you and me.'

'Is this a personal thing or work?'

'Both.'

'I don't like open-ended promises, Joe. What's the general area of what we are talking about?'

'Would you rather I didn't raise the matter with you?'

'Not at all, Joe. I just don't want to be giving promises that I'll do or not do something without knowing what I'm committing myself to.' He paused. 'I've known you too long not to realise that you wouldn't be here unless you thought it was necessary.'

'It's a matter of putting a certain part of the record straight.'

'Part of your record . . .?'

'Mine and one other person's record.'

'To that person's disadvantage?'

'No. Just to my disadvantage.'

'Joe, I don't want to play twenty questions. What are we talking about?'

'I did something way way back that I've come to regret. I put the organisation above human relationships. I wish today that I had acted differently.'

'Does anybody else know about this?'

'Only the other person concerned.'

'Is he gunning for you now?'

'No. He knew what I was doing at the time and he agreed to it. There's no come-back of any kind. Except my conscience.'

Sir Peter looked at Shapiro's solid, four-square face and saw the anguish in the eyes.

'OK, Joe. It's just between you and me.'

'It's about Phoenix. Summers.' He paused. 'He's my son.'

For several minutes Sir Peter was silent and then he said quietly, 'Tell me all about it, Joe. I don't understand yet but I understand well enough how tormented you must be. Just take your time. There's no hurry.'

'When I was a kid in Moscow my protector was a man named Zagorsky. He was tried for treason and I thought

222

he was dead. About nineteen forty-three or forty-four we met accidentally, in London. He was an officer at the Soviet Military Mission under an assumed name. We talked for a couple of hours that night. He didn't know that the Bolsheviks had murdered my wife and abducted my son. He was genuinely upset about it.'

'Did you report any of this?'

'Major Johnson knew about my wife and son. No I didn't mention our talk. He was going to leave the Mission. It wasn't significant.'

'Carry on.'

'In nineteen forty-seven when I was at 21 AG I got a message that a line-crosser was asking to see me. When I talked with him he said Zagorsky had sent him to me to pay off a debt. He had told the young man, who was brought up in a Soviet orphanage, just enough about his background to tell me. The young man had no idea of the significance of what he was telling me. But I did. He was my son.'

'That must have been quite a shock, Joe.'

'It was. I'd always had him in my mind as a baby. It sounds terrible but I found I didn't have the right feeling for him. He was a real nice fellow – but that was all.'

'What happened?'

'I never told him that he was my son. I got false papers for him and he joined the British Army. Because of his intelligence and his languages he was transferred into the Intelligence Corps. Then, as you know, he was transferred to us, to SIS, because he was a fluent Russian speaker. When Hodgkins was looking for a volunteer to be infil-trated into Poland he volunteered. I'd not seen him more than half a dozen times in all that time but it fell to me to provide his legend and documentation. I did it all very, very carefully. The only thing I did that was out of line was to tell him that I knew that his mother had been murdered by Bolsheviks. I showed him the old cuttings from the Berlin newspaper.' He paused. 'I shouldn't have done that. Not as a father. It was unforgivable. It was

223

baiting a trap. And it wasn't even necessary. He'd got all the guts you needed. I put the Polish documents in his mother's family name – Kretski. His British passport and his papers were in my real name of Summers.' Shapiro took a deep breath. 'That's it, Peter. That's about it. I might as well have cut his throat.'

'There's nothing more than that?'

'Maybe just one last thing for the record.'

'Tell me.'

'When I went to Washington to try and persuade them to exchange Abel for Phoenix there was a problem. The CIA had discussed a possible exchange with Abel and he said he would refuse to be part of an exchange. I asked if I could talk to Abel. I'm not sure why but I thought I could persuade him.' Shapiro took a deep breath. 'When we met at the prison it was unbelievable. Colonel Abel was my old friend Zagorsky. That's how he came to agree to the exchange.'

'How is your son now?'

'Physically he's not too bad. They say he'll improve. But mentally he's in a bad way. The quacks say there's nothing clinically or surgically that they can do.'

'Don't they hold out any hope?'

'You know doctors, Peter. Yes. Plenty of hope. Could come all right in a few years. Even over-night. But the prognosis is pessimistic.'

'And you feel you are obliged to take him over?'

'I've no doubt about that. He's my son. It may not feel like it. But he is. That's the least I can do for him.'

'What can you do?'

'Just be around. Wake when he has his nightmares. Hold his hand when he starts screaming. Pray for his soul. And mine.' Sir Peter noticed the quaver in Shapiro's voice and decided that practicalities were the best cure.

'Let's deal with the practicalities first, Joe. You can leave the service in two months' time. I say two months so that we can put you up to full colonel in Part Two orders and your pension will go up accordingly. Early retirement will not affect your pension. It amounts to taking years of accrued leave. I'll see to that.

'So far as your son is concerned, he can be back-dated as a major from when he was caught. His disabilities came on active service so there will be an increased pension for him. His medical bills will be paid by the department and I'll arrange a bounty payment so that there will be enough to buy a house.

'I hope that will relieve you of the day-to-day worries we all have. But I'm worried about you.'

'In what way?'

'You've got a guilt complex, my friend. And like all those things they're never founded on fact but on fantasy. The more rational the man is normally, the wider and deeper the complex.'

'So?'

'Let's look at the chicken's entrails, Joe. Your son was forcibly taken away and there was nothing you could have done to get him back.'

'I could have offered to go back to Moscow if he was released.'

'And who would have cared for him after you'd died in a Gulag camp? Nobody. And then when you saw him again after over twenty years you couldn't relate to a healthy young man when all those years in your mind he was a baby. Irrational maybe but I suspect it's par for the course. And you had no family or anyone else around you to support you and take some of the load. So you did what you could for him.'

'And then sent him to his death.'

'Did you know that Hodgkins was looking for a volunteer?'

'No.'

'Did you suggest to your boy that he should volunteer?'

'No.'

'And when it was all cut and dried and put on your plate to provide his cover did you do it to the best of your ability?'

225

'Of course I did.'

'And is it fair to say that if you had not been his father and an old friend of Abel Zagorsky he would still be in the labour camp or in his grave?'

'It's possible.'

'Joe. Don't be so stupid. You know it is so. When you were that small boy, a cabin-boy on a broken-down merchant ship, you were about to be sucked up by a whirlwind that was sweeping over Europe. Was that the fault of a teenage boy, for God's sake?'

'I appreciate what you've said. I know that it's meant to be helpful but it still leaves me as a very poor specimen of a man.'

'Oh, for Christ's sake, Joe. With a mind like yours, how can you twist the facts so remorselessly? If you were my father I should be very proud of you. And I mean that. Wipe this blackness out of your mind. You've got much to do for that young man. Don't give up your strength to this ridiculous farrago of guilt. If you still feel you have a debt to pay then for God's sake pay it the only way you can. Your usual way, with guts and self-confidence.'

It was Gavrilov from Special Service-I who de-briefed the man whom the world knew as Colonel Abel. They got on well together. Much the same age as one another, worldly-wise so far as Soviets can be, they met almost every day for nearly two years. There was no hidden recorder. It was lying there, turning slowly, quite openly on the table, the latest Uher, bought in West Berlin.

Reel after reel went to the evaluation unit who sent copies of significant sections to other departments and sections of the KGB.

Zagorsky had been given a pleasant apartment over-looking the river. Two rooms and the usual facilities, and a middle-aged lady who cleaned up the place every day. It wasn't an onerous duty but she did sometimes complain about the tangle of wires that sprawled onto the floor from his hi-fi and short-wave receiver.

226

His wants were not extravagant and most of them were easily and willingly provided. In the first summer Zagorsky and Gavrilov took a simple meal every day in a small restaurant within sight of the KGB HQ. They played middle-grade chess and exchanged reminiscences of other cities they had both known in the Soviet Union and abroad. They both confessed to a liking for Paris as a permanent home but neither of them had ever been there.

It was after one of those protracted meals that Gavrilov said, with a smile, 'We were amused when we saw the newspaper cuttings about your trial and it mentioned the coded messages that were supposed to be letters from your loving wife and daughter.'

Zagorsky shrugged. 'Who wrote those damn things?'

'There was a team. When it was decided to use that format for coded messages we got in a lady novelist and we created this little family for you, like a radio serial.'

Zagorsky smiled. 'It was well done. It influenced people. It even made me feel homesick when they read them out in court.'

'We heard that when the pilot's family were pressing for an exchange that you weren't very happy about it. Why was that?'

Zagorsky looked for a few moments at the people walking in the sunshine and then he looked at Gavrilov.

'Off the record or on the record?'

'Off. Nobody's ever raised the point. I was just curious, that's all.'

'First of all I was disappointed that Moscow hadn't offered an exchange for me. The embassy didn't contact me. Nobody. I was just left to rot. I hadn't talked to the Americans. The press made that clear. So I took it as a sign.'

'A sign of what?'

'That Moscow didn't particularly want me to come back so long as I wasn't talking to the CIA. Then out of the blue is the stuff in the newspapers about an exchange with young Powers.' Zagorsky shrugged. 'You get rather paranoid when you've been in prison for years. Years with no contact with my own people and my own country. Virtually the only friendly contacts I had were from the people who put me in jail.

'So when there is a suggestion about an exchange I am well aware that the initiative did not come from Moscow but from the pilot's parents and I asked myself what sort of reception I would get when I returned to Moscow.' Zagorsky smiled at Gavrilov. 'As you know, with a few exceptions it was not a very enthusiastic welcome.' He sighed. 'After all those years of risks and difficulties I have heard people suggest that my mission in the USA was a failure.' Zagorsky shook his head. 'It no longer angers me. It no longer disappoints me. All I ask . . . is to be left in peace.'

'That's no problem, Zag. When the de-briefing is over you'll have your apartment and the *dacha* and all the privileges you're entitled to.'

'We'll see, comrade. We'll see.'

'You don't trust them, do you?'

Zagorsky just smiled as he waved to the waiter for more coffee.

The de-briefing was virtually completed by mid-April and Gavrilov was no longer a daily visitor. Perhaps one short visit a week to tidy up the loose ends in his de-briefing, but no more. Zagorsky still went to the same restaurant for lunch but it wasn't the same on his own. From time to time he saw KGB officers whom he knew from the old days. They waved and smiled but they never stopped to talk or join him at his table. And being long experienced in the ways of the KGB he knew that it would always be like that. He had spent years in the West, virtually unsupervised, independent and surviving. And that made him suspect. To the KGB he was contaminated. It wasn't personal. It applied to anybody who had lived independently in the West. Who knew what they might have been up to? And in any case they were men who now knew about the West. Knew the Soviet lies and knew what freedom was like. The experience didn't necessarily make them pro-Western. There were many things about life in the West that they found abhorrent. But whatever their feelings they knew too much about the lies and fake promises to the people that kept the Bolshevik machine in power. They were not officially ostracised. Nobody was ordered to avoid them. But people knew the system and they didn't need to be told. There was a KGB word for it. Sanitisation.

Zagorsky knew the system too and he didn't resent his treatment. He understood the motives, but it didn't stop him from being lonely. Gradually his outside forays were reduced to a brief daily walk for exercise and then back to his rooms. It was not unlike his life in New York. But he missed the people and he missed the talk. Being a patriot he spent no time wondering if his life was just reward· for his services to his country. He left no will or last testament and it was the cleaning lady who found his body one morning. He was still sitting crouched in the leather armchair and there was jazz coming from the short-wave receiver which was tuned to 'The Voice of America'.

The meeting between Volnov and Gavrilov about the man who had used the name of Gordon Lonsdale took place in a *dacha* about ten miles east of Moscow. It was held at the *dacha*, not for any security reason but merely because Volnov didn't want to spoil his weekend in the country. He was in his sixties and he didn't like his routine being disturbed. Especially for a man he positively disliked. Gavrilov too disliked Lonsdale but he was stuck with the responsibility of deciding what should be done·with him. He sensed that his compromise proposal was not going to be acceptable to the older man. But he could see no alternative that would be tolerable to those who wanted Lonsdale to be given public honours.

Volnov folded his arms and leaned back against the cushions on the couch.

'Why all the fuss about the man? He was never in danger. The worst that could happen to him was a prison sentence. We exchanged him for the Englishman Lynne or Wynne, whatever his name was. He's back here without a hair of his head disturbed. So why the circus?'

'He did a good job for us.'

'Rubbish. The fool was caught. His network in London was handed to him on a plate from Moscow. He was just a glorified messenger-boy.'

'It would help him with his family problems.'

'That woman's right – his wife. I saw all that translation of the English newspapers. "I was spy's mistress says Natasha something or other".' His face was flushed as he looked at Gavrilov. 'All those foreign whores he slept with. She should be allowed to divorce him if that's what she wants.'

'Then we have another scandal on our hands.'

'No need to announce it. It can be kept quiet. You can warn the woman not to talk.'

'It's not as easy as that, Comrade Volnov.'

'Why not?'

'It would be bad for the morale of others we send overseas if we didn't support Konrad Molody.'

'Let it be a lesson to them. Don't screw foreign tarts. They expect their wives to be faithful but they live like brothel-keepers themselves.'

'The woman herself did not live an entirely blameless life while he was away.'

'So. Let them stew in their own juice, the two of them.'

'The naval intelligence people were very pleased with what he sent back.'

'So. It was the others who took the risks. The Cohens and the English couple. They did the work and they're still in jail. Molody just passed it on.'

'That's all that most of them do.'

'Rubbish.' He paused. 'Anyway, what is it you want to do?'

230

'I've suggested that he writes a book. An autobiography. In English so that it can be sold in the West.'

'For what purpose?'

'So that the English and American public can see how inefficient their intelligence services are.'

'They don't give a damn one way or another.'

'The propaganda section say that it could cause a lot of embarrassment for London and Washington.'

'And Molody is the master-spy who deceives them all. The gallant hero.'

'Of course.'

'And that would keep him happy? And feed his ego?'

'Yes. We should control every word of it of course.'

Volnov shrugged, impatiently. 'Do it then, if that's what you want. But mark my words. There are to be no flags and no heroics in Moscow for Molody.'

'Right, comrade.'

'Don't look so pleased with yourself, Gavrilov. You're wasting your time bothering with that arrogant little kulak.'

Reino Hayhanen died in an unexplained car-crash on the Pennsylvania Turnpike.

Joe Shapiro bought a cottage in Northumberland. Near Bamburgh, within sight of the sea and within easy walking distance of the long sandy beaches. Except for a few weeks in summer the beautiful beaches were deserted and Shapiro and his son walked daily along the coast in all kinds of weather.

Shapiro had chosen that part of the world because he wanted to be away from people. Sir Peter had arranged for medical treatment for John Summers by a Newcastle doctor who was ex-Special Operations Executive and whose discretion could be trusted. He had not been told everything, but enough to understand the background of the man he was treating. When it was impossible to avoid contact with local people they were told that John

Summers was a polio victim, an explanation that was readily accepted.

As the months went by the nightmares were less frequent but there was no improvement in speech or hearing. At a two-day check-up just before the Easter holiday Shapiro was told that tests showed that there was a strong indication that his son could now definitely hear sounds at certain frequencies. But what had seemed like good news was dashed by the consultant's opinion that the tests also indicated that there was no likelihood of John Summers ever recognising speech. There appeared to be some gap in the nervous system that meant that while the ear itself reacted to certain sounds there was no link to the brain itself, and therefore no recognition of the sounds. Although it was cautiously and considerately put it was made clear that Shapiro could expect no improvement. He would best accept that his son's life would continue to be physically normal but mentally retarded.

Shapiro's life was devoted entirely to his son. A life of routine drudgery as nurse, guardian and housekeeper that he bore with a stoicism that was a mixture of irrational guilt and resignation, and a genuine affection for the human being who had been so ruthlessly destroyed by evil men. There were times when his spirit flagged and he classed himself as one of the evil men.

In January of the second year they had to go for another consultation. This time in London. The journey by train from Newcastle had been such a strain on his son that he decided that it would be better to take a plane back to Newcastle. The short journey had been uneventful despite the take-off being delayed because of the bad weather.

When they touched down at Newcastle they were warned about slippery steps because of the snow, and snow swirled around them as they walked towards the terminal building. They were almost there when his son grabbed his arm trying to stop him from walking into the building. As he turned to look at him his son was shaking his head, grunting as he sometimes did when he was disturbed. And then, as if by some miracle he heard the words. Words in Russian. A jumble of half-finished sentences. Swear words, curses, violent protests and then, his chest heaving, his eyes staring John Summers gasped, 'Where in God's name am I? What am I doing here? Where are the guards?'

Shapiro spoke, also in Russian. 'You're safe, Jan. You're free. There are no guards. We're going home to the cottage.'

'They are waiting for me inside. We didn't land at Sheremetyevo. They know. They've got a photograph.' He looked away, towards the people inside the well-lit terminal building. Then he looked back at Shapiro. 'This isn't Moscow . . . not . . . I don't feel well.' There were tears coursing down his cheeks and Shapiro put his arm around him. 'We're in England, Jan. There's nothing to worry about. The car is in the car-park. We're going home.'

As Shapiro drove up the A1 to Alnwick he listened to the flow of words from the back seat. Sometimes Russian, sometimes Polish. And finally in English. Strange juxtapositions of the words of hymns, girls' names and endearments, a short burst of laughter and then quiet heavy breathing as John Summers slept.

They sat together in the cottage until it was getting light the next morning. As they talked Shapiro picked his way carefully through the minefield of a brain that had too much to unload. But as he sat there with the man who was his son he knew that the long slog was over. It was going to be all right. His son could hear and speak and sometimes he stopped and replied to a question. All he had to do was help that wounded psyche get back to health and peace and then, by God, he could make amends.